By Evelyn Waugh

Novels
DECLINE AND FALL
VILE BODIES
BLACK MISCHIEF
A HANDFUL OF DUST
SCOOP
PUT OUT MORE FLAGS
WORK SUSPENDED
BRIDESHEAD REVISITED
SCOTT-KING'S MODERN EUROPE
THE LOVED ONE
HELENA
MEN AT ARMS
LOVE AMONG THE RUINS
OFFICERS AND GENTLEMEN
UNCONDITIONAL SURRENDER
THE ORDEAL OF GILBERT
   PINFOLD

Biography
ROSSETTI
EDMUND CAMPION
MSGR. RONALD KNOX

Autobiography
A LITTLE LEARNING

Travel
LABELS
REMOTE PEOPLE
NINETY-TWO DAYS
WAUGH IN ABYSSINIA
ROBBERY UNDER LAW
WHEN THE GOING WAS GOOD
A TOURIST IN AFRICA

Short Stories
CHARLES RYDER'S SCHOOLDAYS AND OTHER STORIES
BASIL SEAL RIDES AGAIN

Journalism
A LITTLE ORDER
(EDITED BY DONAT GALLAGHER)

CHARLES RYDER'S SCHOOLDAYS
AND OTHER STORIES

CHARLES RYDER'S SCHOOLDAYS

and Other Stories

by
EVELYN WAUGH

LITTLE, BROWN AND COMPANY • BOSTON • TORONTO

FIRST EDITION

All stories excepting "Charles Ryder's Schooldays" have appeared
in a limited edition published in 1936 under the title *Mr. Loveday's Little Outing*.

Lines from "The Bells of Heaven" from *Poems* by Ralph
Hodgson, copyright 1917 by Macmillan Publishing Co., Inc.,
renewed 1945 by Ralph Hodgson.

BP

PRINTED IN THE UNITED STATES OF AMERICA

CONTENTS

MR. LOVEDAY'S LITTLE OUTING

"YOU will not find your father greatly changed," remarked Lady Moping, as the car turned into the gates of the County Asylum.

"Will he be wearing a uniform?" asked Angela.

"No, dear, of course not He is receiving the very best attention."

It was Angela's first visit and it was being made at her own suggestion.

Ten years had passed since the showery day in late summer when Lord Moping had been taken away; a day of confused but bitter memories for her; the day of Lady Moping's annual garden party, always bitter, confused that day by the caprice of the weather which, remaining clear and brilliant with promise until the arrival of the first guests, had suddenly blackened into a squall. There had been a scuttle for cover; the marquee had capsized; a frantic carrying of cushions and chairs; a table-cloth lofted to the boughs of the monkey-puzzler, fluttering in the rain; a bright period and the cautious emergence of guests onto the soggy lawns ; another squall ; another twenty minutes of sunshine. It had been an abominable afternoon, culminating at about six o'clock in her father's attempted suicide.

Lord Moping habitually threatened suicide on the occasion of the garden party ; that year he had been found black in the face, hanging by his braces in the orangery ; some neighbours, who were sheltering there from the rain, set him on his feet again, and before dinner a van had called for him. Since then Lady Moping had paid seasonal calls at the asylum and returned in time for tea, rather reticent of her experience.

Many of her neighbours were inclined to be critical of Lord Moping's accommodation. He was not, of course, an ordinary inmate. He lived in a separate wing of the asylum, specially devoted to the segregation of wealthier lunatics. These were given every consideration which their foibles permitted. They might choose their own clothes (many indulged in the liveliest fancies), smoke the most expensive brands of cigars, and on the anniversaries of their certification entertain any other inmates for whom they had an attachment, to private dinner parties.

The fact remained, however, that it was far from being the most expensive kind of institution ; the uncompromising address,

"COUNTY HOME FOR MENTAL DEFECTIVES" stamped across the note-paper, worked on the uniforms of their attendants, painted, even, upon a prominent hoarding at the main entrance, suggested the lowest associations. From time to time, with less or more tact, her friends attempted to bring to Lady Moping's notice particulars of seaside nursing homes, of 'qualified practitioners with large private grounds suitable for the charge of nervous or difficult cases', but she accepted them lightly; when her son came of age he might make any changes that he thought fit; meanwhile she felt no inclination to relax her economical régime; her husband had betrayed her basely on the one day in the year when she looked for loyal support, and was far better off than he deserved.

A few lonely figures in great-coats were shuffling and loping about the park.

"Those are the lower class lunatics," observed Lady Moping. "There is a very nice little flower garden for people like your father. I sent them some cuttings last year."

They drove past the blank, yellow brick façade to the doctor's private entrance and were received by him in the 'visitors room', set aside for interviews of this kind. The window was protected on the inside by bars and wire netting; there was no fireplace; when Angela nervously attempted to move her chair further from the radiator, she found that it was screwed to the floor.

"Lord Moping is quite ready to see you," said the doctor.

"How is he?"

"Oh, very well, very well indeed, I'm glad to say. He had rather a nasty cold some time ago, but apart from that his condition is excellent. He spends a lot of his time in writing."

They heard a shuffling, skipping sound approaching along the flagged passage. Outside the door a high peevish voice, which Angela recognized as her father's, said: "I haven't the time, I tell you. Let them come back later."

A gentler tone, with a slight rural burr, replied, "Now come along. It is a purely formal audience. You need stay no longer than you like."

Then the door was pushed open (it had no lock or fastening) and Lord Moping came into the room. He was attended by an elderly little man with full white hair and an expression of great kindness.

" That is Mr. Loveday who acts as Lord Moping's attendant."

" Secretary," said Lord Moping. He moved with a jogging gait and shook hands with his wife.

" This is Angela. You remember Angela, don't you ? "

" No, I can't say that I do. What does she want ? "

" We just came to see you."

" Well, you have come at an exceedingly inconvenient time. I am very busy. Have you typed out that letter to the Pope yet, Loveday ? "

" No, my lord. If you remember, you asked me to look up the figures about the Newfoundland fisheries first ? "

" So I did. Well, it is fortunate, as I think the whole letter will have to be redrafted. A great deal of new information has come to light since luncheon. A great deal . . . You see, my dear, I am fully occupied." He turned his restless, quizzical eyes upon Angela. " I suppose you have come about the Danube. Well, you must come again later. Tell them it will be all right, quite all right, but I have not had time to give my full attention to it. Tell them that."

" Very well, Papa."

" Anyway," said Lord Moping rather

petulantly, "it is a matter of secondary importance. There is the Elbe and the Amazon and the Tigris to be dealt with first, eh, Loveday ? . . . *Danube* indeed. Nasty little river. I'd only call it a stream myself. Well, can't stop, nice of you to come. I would do more for you if I could, but you see how I'm fixed. Write to me about it. That's it. *Put it in black and white.*"

And with that he left the room.

" You see," said the doctor, " he is in excellent condition. He is putting on weight, eating and sleeping excellently. In fact, the whole tone of his system is above reproach."

The door opened again and Loveday returned.

" Forgive my coming back, sir, but I was afraid that the young lady might be upset at his Lordship's not knowing her. You mustn't mind him, miss. Next time he'll be very pleased to see you. It's only to-day he's put out on account of being behindhand with his work. You see, sir, all this week I've been helping in the library and I haven't been able to get all his Lordship's reports typed out. And he's got muddled with his card index. That's all it is. He doesn't mean any harm."

" What a nice man," said Angela, when Loveday had gone back to his charge.

14

"Yes. I don't know what we should do without old Loveday. Everybody loves him, staff and patients alike."

"I remember him well. It's a great comfort to know that you are able to get such good warders," said Lady Moping; "people who don't know, say such foolish things about asylums."

"Oh, but Loveday isn't a warder," said the doctor.

"You don't mean he's cuckoo, too?" said Angela.

The doctor corrected her.

"He is an *inmate*. It is rather an interesting case. He has been here for thirty-five years."

"But I've never seen anyone saner," said Angela.

"He certainly has that air," said the doctor, "and in the last twenty years we have treated him as such. He is the life and soul of the place. Of course he is not one of the private patients, but we allow him to mix freely with them. He plays billiards excellently, does conjuring tricks at the concert, mends their gramophones, valets them, helps them in their crossword puzzles and various—er—hobbies. We allow them to give him small tips for services rendered, and he must by now have amassed quite a little fortune. He has a way with even the most troublesome of them. An invaluable man about the place."

" Yes, but why is he here ? "

" Well, it is rather sad. When he was a very young man he killed somebody—a young woman quite unknown to him, whom he knocked off her bicycle and then throttled. He gave himself up immediately afterwards and has been here ever since."

" But surely he is perfectly safe now. Why is he not let out ? "

" Well, I suppose if it was to anyone's interest, he would be. He has no relatives except a step-sister who lives in Plymouth. She used to visit him at one time, but she hasn't been for years now. He's perfectly happy here and I can assure you *we* aren't going to take the first steps in turning him out. He's far too useful to us."

" But it doesn't seem fair," said Angela.

" Look at your father," said the doctor. " He'd be quite lost without Loveday to act as his secretary."

" It doesn't seem fair."

2

Angela left the asylum, oppressed by a sense of injustice. Her mother was unsympathetic.

" Think of being locked up in a looney bin all one's life."

" He attempted to hang himself in the orangery," replied Lady Moping, " *in front of the Chester-Martins.*"

" I don't mean Papa. I mean Mr. Loveday."

" I don't think I know him."

" Yes, the looney they have put to look after papa."

" Your father's secretary. A very decent sort of man, I thought, and eminently suited to his work."

Angela left the question for the time, but returned to it again at luncheon on the following day.

" Mums, what does one have to do to get people out of the bin ? "

" The bin ? Good gracious, child, I hope that you do not anticipate your father's return *here.*"

" No, no. Mr. Loveday."

" Angela, you seem to me to be totally bemused. I see it was a mistake to take you with me on our little visit yesterday."

After luncheon Angela disappeared to the library and was soon immersed in the lunacy laws as represented in the encyclopædia.

She did not re-open the subject with her mother, but a fortnight later, when there was a question of taking some pheasants over to her father for his eleventh Certification Party she showed an unusual willingness to run over with them. Her mother was occupied with other interests and noticed nothing suspicious.

Angela drove her small car to the asylum, and after delivering the game, asked for Mr. Loveday. He was busy at the time making a crown for one of his companions who expected hourly to be anointed Emperor of Brazil, but he left his work and enjoyed several minutes' conversation with her. They spoke about her father's health and spirits. After a time Angela remarked, " Don't you ever want to get away ? "

Mr. Loveday looked at her with his gentle, blue-grey eyes. " I've got very well used to the life, miss. I'm fond of the poor people here, and I think that several of them are quite fond of me. At least, I think they would miss me if I were to go."

" But don't you ever think of being free again ? "

" Oh yes, miss, I think of it—almost all the time I think of it."

" What would you do if you got out ? There must be *something* you would sooner do than stay here."

The old man fidgeted uneasily. " Well, miss, it sounds ungrateful, but I can't deny I should welcome a little outing, once, before I get too old to enjoy it. I expect we all have our secret ambitions, and there *is* one thing I often wish I could do. You mustn't ask me what. . . It wouldn't take long. But I do feel that if I had done it, just for a day, an afternoon even, then I would die quiet. I could settle down again easier, and devote myself to the poor crazed people here with a better heart. Yes, I do feel that."

There were tears in Angela's eyes that afternoon as she drove away. " He *shall* have his little outing, bless him," she said.

3

From that day onwards for many weeks Angela had a new purpose in life. She moved about the ordinary routine of her home with an abstracted air and an unfamiliar, reserved courtesy which greatly disconcerted Lady Moping.

" I believe the child's in love. I only pray that it isn't that uncouth Egbertson boy."

She read a great deal in the library, she cross-examined any guests who had pretensions to legal or medical knowledge, she showed extreme goodwill to old Sir Roderick Lane-Foscote, their Member. The names "alienist," "barrister" or "government official" now had for her the glamour that formerly surrounded film actors and professional wrestlers. She was a woman with a cause, and before the end of the hunting season she had triumphed. Mr. Loveday achieved his liberty.

The doctor at the asylum showed reluctance but no real opposition. Sir Roderick wrote to the Home Office. The necessary papers were signed, and at last the day came when Mr. Loveday took leave of the home where he had spent such long and useful years.

His departure was marked by some ceremony. Angela and Sir Roderick Lane-Foscote sat with the doctors on the stage of the gymnasium. Below them were assembled everyone in the institution who was thought to be stable enough to endure the excitement.

Lord Moping, with a few suitable expressions of regret, presented Mr. Loveday on behalf of the wealthier lunatics with a gold cigarette case ; those who supposed themselves to be emperors showered him with decorations and titles of honour. The warders gave him a silver watch and many of the non-paying inmates were in tears on the day of the presentation.

The doctor made the main speech of the afternoon. " Remember," he remarked, " that you leave behind you nothing but our warmest good wishes. You are bound to us by ties that none will forget. Time will only deepen our sense of debt to you. If at any time in the future you should grow tired of your life in the world, there will always be a welcome for you here. Your post will be open."

A dozen or so variously afflicted lunatics hopped and skipped after him down the drive until the iron gates opened and Mr. Loveday stepped into his freedom. His small trunk had already gone to the station ; he elected to walk. He had been reticent about his plans, but he was well provided with money, and the general impression was that he would go to London and enjoy himself a little before visiting his step-sister in Plymouth.

It was to the surprise of all that he returned within two hours of his liberation. He was smiling whimsically, a gentle, self-regarding smile of reminiscence.

" I have come back," he informed the doctor. " I think that now I shall be here for good."

" But, Loveday, what a short holiday. I'm afraid that you have hardly enjoyed yourself at all."

" Oh yes, sir, thank you, sir, I've enjoyed

myself *very much*. I'd been promising myself one little treat, all these years. It was short, sir, but *most* enjoyable. Now I shall be able to settle down again to my work here without any regrets."

Half a mile up the road from the asylum gates, they later discovered an abandoned bicycle. It was a lady's machine of some antiquity. Quite near it in the ditch lay the strangled body of a young woman, who, riding home to her tea, had chanced to overtake Mr. Loveday, as he strode along, musing on his opportunities.

BY SPECIAL REQUEST

An alternative ending to *A Handful of Dust*

This was used in the serialised version. It takes the place of Chapters V, VI and VII and would begin at page 241 of the book. The entire Brazilian incident is thus omitted. Tony Last leaves London on the breakdown of his wife's arrangements for divorce, and goes on a prolonged and leisurely cruise.

CHAPTER FIVE

THE NEXT WINTER

I

THE liner came into harbour at
Southampton, late in the afternoon.
They had left the sun three days
behind them; after the Azores there had
been a high sea running; in the Channel a
white mist. Tony had been awake all night,
disturbed by the fog signals and the uncertainty of home-coming.

They berthed alongside the quay. Tony
leant on the rail looking for his chauffeur.
He had cabled to Hetton that he was to be
met and would drive straight home. He
wanted to see the new bathrooms. Half the
summer workmen had been at Hetton. There
would be several changes to greet him.

It had been an uneventful excursion. Not
for Tony were the ardours of serious travel,
desert or jungle, mountain or pampas; he
had no inclination to kill big game or survey

unmapped tributaries. He had left England because, in the circumstances, it seemed the correct procedure, a convention hallowed in fiction and history by generations of disillusioned husbands. He had put himself in the hands of a travel agency and for lazy months had pottered from island to island in the West Indies, lunching at Government Houses, drinking swizzles on club verandahs, achieving an easy popularity at Captains' tables; he had played deck quoits and ping-pong, had danced on deck and driven with new acquaintances, on well-laid roads amid tropical vegetation. Now he was home again. He had thought less and less of Brenda during the passing weeks.

Presently he identified his chauffeur among the sparse population of the quay. The man came on board and took charge of the luggage. The car was waiting on the other side of the customs sheds.

The chauffeur said, " Shall I have the big trunk sent on by train ? "

" There's plenty of room for it behind the car, isn't there ? "

" Well, hardly, sir. Her ladyship has a lot of luggage with her."

" Her ladyship ? "

" Yes, sir. Her ladyship is waiting in the

car. She telegraphed that I was to pick her up at the hotel."

" I see. And she has a lot of luggage ? "

" Yes, sir, an uncommon lot."

" Well . . . perhaps you *had* better send the trunks by train."

" Very good, sir."

So Tony went out to the car alone, while his chauffeur was seeing to the trunks.

Brenda was in the back, shrunk into the corner. She had taken off her hat—a very small knitted hat, clipped with a brooch he had given her some years ago—and was holding it in her lap. There was deep twilight inside the car. She looked up without moving her head.

" Darling," she said, " your boat was *very* late."

" Yes, we had fog in the channel."

" I got here last night. The people in the office said you'd be in early this morning."

" Yes, we *are* late."

" You can never tell with ships, can you ? " said Brenda.

There was a pause. Then she said, " Aren't you going to come in ? "

" There's a fuss about the luggage."

" Blake will see to that."

" He's sending it by train."

"Yes, I thought he would have to. I'm sorry I brought so much . . . You see, I brought everything. I've turned against that flat . . . It never quite lost the smell. I thought it was just newness, but it got worse. You know—*radiator smell*. So what with one thing and another I thought, how about giving it up."

Then the chauffeur came back. He had settled everything about the luggage.

"Well, we'd better start right away."

"Very good, sir."

Tony got in beside Brenda, and the chauffeur shut the door on them. They ran through the streets of Southampton and out into the country. The lamps were already alight behind the windows they passed.

"How did you know I was coming this afternoon?"

"I *thought* you were coming this morning. Jock told me."

"I didn't expect to see you."

"Jock said you'd be surprised."

"How *is* Jock?"

"Something awful happened to him, but I can't remember what. I think it was to do with politics—or it may have been a girl. I can't remember."

They sat far apart, each in a corner. Tony

was very tired after his sleepless night. His eyes were heavy and the lights hurt them when the car passed through a bright little town.

" Have you been having a lovely time ? "

" Yes.   Have you ? "

" No, rather lousy really.   But I don't expect you want to hear about that."

" What are your plans ? "

" Vague.   What are yours ? "

" Vague."

And then in the close atmosphere and gentle motion of the car, Tony fell asleep.   He slept for two and a half hours, with his face half hidden in the collar of his overcoat.   Once, as they stopped at a level crossing, he half woke up and asked, deep down in the tweed, " Are we there ? "

" No, darling.   *Miles* more."

And then he fell asleep again and woke to find them hooting at the lodge gates.   He woke, too, to find that the question which neither he nor Brenda had asked, was answered. This should have been a crisis ; his destinies had been at his control ; there had been things to say, a decision to make, affecting every hour of his future life.   *And he had fallen asleep.*

Ambrose was on the drawbridge to greet

them. " Good evening, my lady. Good evening, sir. I hope you have had an agreeable voyage, sir."

" Most agreeable, thank you, Ambrose. Everything quite all right here ? "

" Everything *quite* all right, sir. There are one or two small things, but perhaps I had better mention them in the morning."

" Yes, in the morning."

" Your correspondence is all in the library, sir."

" Thank you. I'll see to all that to-morrow."

They went into the great hall and upstairs. A large log fire was burning in Guinevere.

" The men only left last week, sir. I think you will find their work quite satisfactory."

While his suitcase was being unpacked, Tony and Brenda examined the new bathrooms. Tony turned on the taps.

" I haven't had the furnace lighted, sir. But it was lit the other day and the result was quite satisfactory."

" Let's not change," said Brenda.

" No. We'll have dinner right away, Ambrose."

During dinner, Tony talked about his trip ; of the people he had met, and the charm of the scenery, the improvidence of the negro population, the fine flavour of the tropical fruits, the varying hospitality of the different Governors.

"I wonder if we could grow Avocado pears, here, under glass," he said.

Brenda did not say very much. Once he asked her, "Have you been away at all?" and she replied "Me? No. London all the time."

"How is everybody?"

"I didn't see many people. Polly's in America."

And that set Tony talking about the excellent administration in Haiti. "They've made a new place of it," he said.

After dinner they sat in the library. Tony surveyed the substantial pile of letters that had accumulated for him in his absence. "I can't do anything about that to-night," he said. "I'm so tired."

"Yes, let's go to bed soon."

There was a pause, and it was then that Brenda said, "You aren't still in a rage with me, are you? . . . over that nonsense with Mr. Beaver, I mean?"

"I don't know that I was ever in a rage."

"Oh yes you were. Just at the end you were, before you went away."

Tony did not answer.

"You aren't in a rage, *are* you? I hoped

31

you weren't, when you went to sleep in the car."

Instead of answering, Tony asked, " What's become of Beaver ? "

" It's rather a sad story, do you really want to hear it ? "

" Yes."

" Well, I come out of it in a very small way. You see, I just couldn't hold him down. He got away almost the same time as you.

" You see, you didn't leave me with very much money, did you ? And that made everything difficult because poor Mr. Beaver hadn't any either. So everything was *most* uncomfortable. . . . And then there was a club he wanted to join—Brown's—and they wouldn't have him in, and for some reason he held *that* against me, because he thought I ought to have made Reggie help more instead of what actually happened, which was that Reggie was the chief one to keep him out. Gentlemen are so funny about their clubs, I should have thought it was heaven to have Mr. Beaver there, but they didn't.

" And then Mrs. Beaver turned against me—she was always an old trout anyway— and I tried to get a job with her shop, but no, she wouldn't have me on account she thought

I was doing harm to Beaver. And then I had a job with Daisy trying to get people to go to her restaurant, but that wasn't any good, and those I got didn't pay their bills.

" So there was I living on bits from the delicatessen shop round the corner, and no friends much except Jenny, and I got to hate her.

" Tony, it was a lousy summer.

" And then, finally, there was an American vamp called Mrs. Rattery—*you know*, the Shameless Blonde. Well, my Mr. Beaver met her and from that moment I was nowhere. Of course she was just his ticket and he was bats about her, only she never seemed to notice him, and every time he met her she forgot she'd seen him before, and that was hard cheese on Beaver, but it didn't make him any more decent to me. And he wore himself to a shadow chasing after her and getting no fun, till finally Mrs. Beaver sent him away and he's got some job to do with her shop buying things in Berlin or Vienna.

" So that's that . . . *Tony*, I believe you're falling asleep again."

" Well, I didn't get any sleep a' all last night."

" Come on, let's go up."

33

2

That winter, shortly before Christmas, Daisy opened another restaurant. Tony and Brenda were in London for the day, so they went there to lunch. It was very full (Daisy's restaurants were often full, but it never seemed to make any effect on the resulting deficit). They went to their table nodding gaily to right and left.

" All the old faces," said Brenda.

A few places away sat Polly Cockpurse and Sybil with two young men.

" Who was that ? "

" Brenda and Tony Last. I wonder what's become of them. They never appear anywhere now."

" They never did much."

" I had an idea they'd split."

" It doesn't look like it."

" Come to think of it, I *do* remember some talk last spring," said Sybil.

" Yes, I remember. Brenda had a fancy for someone quite extraordinary. I can't remember who it was, but I know it was someone quite extraordinary." ·

" Wasn't that her sister Marjorie ? "

" Oh no, *hers* was Robin Beasley."

" Yes, of course . . . Brenda's looking pretty."

" Such a waste. But I don't think she'd ever have the energy now to get away."

At Brenda and Tony's table they were saying, " I wish *you'd* see her."

" No, you *must* see her."

" All right, I'll see her."

Tony had to go and see Mrs. Beaver about the flat. Ever since his return they had been trying to sublet it. Now Mrs. Beaver had informed them that there was a tenant in sight.

So while Brenda was at the doctor's (she was expecting a baby) Tony went round to the shop.

Mrs. Beaver was surrounded with a new sort of lampshade made of cellophane and cork.

" *How* are you, Mr. Last ? " she said, rather formally. " We haven't met since that *delightful* week-end at Hetton."

" I hear you've found a tenant for the flat."

" Yes, I think so. A young cousin of Viola Chasm's. Of course I'm afraid you'll have to make some slight sacrifice. You see the flats have proved *too* popular, if you see what I mean. The demand was so brisk that a great many other firms came into the market and, as a result, rents have fallen. *Everyone* is taking flats of the kind now, but the speculative builders are letting them at competitive rents. The new tenant will only pay two pounds fifteen a week and he insists on its being entirely repainted. *We* will undertake that, of course. I think we can make a very nice job of it for fifty pounds or so."

"You know," said Tony, "I've been thinking. It's rather a useful thing to have— a flat of that kind."

"It is *necessary*," said Mrs. Beaver.

"Exactly. Well I think I shall keep it on. The only trouble is that my wife is inclined to fret a little about the rent. My idea is to use it when I come to London instead of my club. It will be cheaper and a great deal more convenient. But my wife may not see it in that light . . . in fact . . ."

"I *quite* understand."

"I think it would be better if my name didn't appear on that board downstairs."

"Naturally. A number of my tenants are taking the same precaution."

"So that's all right."

"That's quite satisfactory. I daresay you will want some little piece of extra furniture— a writing-table, for instance."

"Yes, I suppose I had better."

" I'll send one round.   I think I know just what will suit you."

The table was delivered a week later.   It cost eighteen pounds ; on the same day there was a new name painted on the board below.

And for the price of the table Mrs. Beaver observed absolute discretion.

Tony met Brenda at Marjorie's house and they caught the evening train together.

" Did you get rid of the flat ? " she asked.

" Yes, that's all settled."

" Mrs. Beaver decent ? "

" *Very* decent."

" So that's the end of that," said Brenda.

And the train sped through the darkness towards Hetton.

CRUISE

LETTERS FROM A YOUNG LADY OF LEISURE

LETTERS FROM A YOUNG LADY OF LEISURE

S.S. *Glory of Greece*

DARLING,
Well I said I would write and so I would have only goodness it was rough so didnt. Now everything is a bit more alright so I will tell you. Well as you know the cruise started at Monte Carlo and when papa and all of us went to Victoria we found that the tickets didnt include the journey there so Goodness how furious he was and said he wouldnt go but Mum said of course we must go and we said that too only papa had changed all his money into Liri or Franks on account of foreigners being so dishonest but he kept a shilling for the porter at Dover being methodical so then he had to change it back again and that set him wrong all the way to Monte Carlo and he wouldnt get me and Bertie a sleeper and wouldnt sleep himself in his through being so angry Goodness how Sad.

Then everything was much more alright

41

tne purser called him Colonel and he likes his cabin so he took Bertie to the casino and he lost and Bertie won and I think Bertie got a bit plastered at least he made a noise going to bed he's in the next cabin as if he were being sick and that was before we sailed. Bertie has got some books on Baroque art on account of his being at Oxford.

Well the first day it was rough and I got up and felt odd in the bath and the soap wouldnt work on account of salt water you see and came into breakfast and there was a list of so many things including steak and onions and there was a corking young man who said we are the only ones down may I sit here and it was going beautifully and he had steak and onions but it was no good I had to go back to bed just when he was saying there was nothing he admired so much about a girl as her being a good sailor goodness how sad.

The thing is not to have a bath and to be very slow in all movements. So next day it was Naples and we saw some Bertie churches and then that bit that got blown up in an earthquake and a poor dog killed they have a plaster cast of him goodness how sad. Papa and Bertie saw some pictures we weren't allowed to see and Bill drew them for me afterwards and Miss P. tried to look too.

I havent told you about Bill and Miss P. have I ? Well Bill is rather old but clean looking and I dont suppose hes very old not really I mean and he's had a very disillusionary life on account of his wife who he says I wont say a word against but she gave him the raspberry with a foreigner and that makes him hate foreigners. Miss P. is called Miss Phillips and is lousy she wears a yachting cap and is a bitch. And the way she makes up to the second officer is no ones business and its clear to the meanest intelligence he hates her but its part of the rules that all the sailors have to pretend to fancy the passengers. Who else is there ? Well a lot of old ones. Papa is having a walk out with one called Lady Muriel something or other who knew uncle Ned. And there is a honeymoon couple very embarrassing. And a clergyman and a lovely pansy with a camera and white suit and lots of families from the industrial north.

So Bertie sends his love too. XXXXXX etc.

Mum bought a shawl and an animal made of lava.

Post-card.

This is a picture of Taormina. Mum bought a shawl here. V. funny because Miss P. got left as shed made chums only with second officer and he wasnt allowed ashore so when it came to getting into cars Miss P. had to pack in with a family from the industrial north.

S.S. *Glory of Greece*

Darling,

Hope you got P.C. from Sicily. The moral of that was not to make chums with sailors though who I've made a chum of is the purser who's different on account he leads a very cynical life with a gramophone in his cabin and as many cocktails as he likes and welsh rabbits sometimes and I said but do you pay for all these drinks but he said no that's all right.

So we have three days at sea which the clergyman said is a good thing as it makes us all friendly but it hasn't made me friendly with Miss P. who won't leave poor Bill alone not taking any more chances of being left alone when she goes ashore. The purser says theres always someone like her on board in fact he says that about everyone except me who he says quite rightly is different goodness how decent.

So there are deck games they are hell. And

the day before we reach Haifa there is to be a
fancy dress dance. Papa is very good at the
deck games expecially one called shuffle board
and eats more than he does in London but I
daresay its alright. You have to hire dresses
for the ball from the barber I mean we do not
you. Miss P. has brought her own. So I've
thought of a v. clever thing at least the purser
suggested it and that is to wear the clothes of
one of the sailors I tried his on and looked a
treat. Poor Miss P.

Bertie is madly unpop. he wont play any of
the games and being plastered the other night
too and tried to climb down a ventilator and
the second officer pulled him out and the old
ones at the captains table look *askance* at him.
New word that. Literary yes ? No ?

So I think the pansy is writing a book he has
a green fountain pen and green ink but I
couldnt see what it was. XXXX Pretty good
about writing you will say and so I am.

Post-card.

This is a photograph of the Holyland and
the famous sea of Gallillee. It is all v. Eastern
with camels. I have a lot to tell you about
the ball. *Such* goings on and will write very

45

soon. Papa went off for the day with Lady M. and came back saying enchanting woman Knows the world.

S.S. Glory of Greece

Darling,

Well the Ball we had to come in to dinner in our clothes and everyone clapped as we came downstairs. So I was pretty late on account of not being able to make up my mind whether to wear the hat and in the end did and looked a corker. Well it was rather a faint clap for me considering so when I looked about there were about twenty girls and some women all dressed like me so how cynical the purser turns out to be. Bertie looked horribly dull as an apache. Mum and Papa were sweet. Miss P. had a ballet dress from the Russian ballet which couldnt have been more unsuitable so we had champagne for dinner and were jolly and they threw paper streamers and I threw mine before it was unrolled and hit Miss P. on the nose. Ha ha. So feeling matey I said to the steward isnt this fun and he said yes for them who hasnt got to clear it up goodness how Sad.

Well of course Bertie was plastered and went a bit far particularly in what he said to Lady M. then he sat in the cynical pursers cabin in the dark and cried so Bill and I found him and Bill gave him some drinks and what you do think he went off with Miss P. and we didnt see either of them again it only shows into what degradation the Demon Drink can drag you him I mean.

Then who should I meet but the young man who had steak and onions on the first morning and is called Robert and said I have been trying to meet you again all the voyage. Then I bitched him a bit goodness how Decent.

Poor Mum got taken up by Bill and he told her all about his wife and how she had disillusioned him with the foreigner so to-morrow we reach Port Said d.v. which is latin in case you didn't know meaning God Willing and all go up the nile and to Cairo for a week.

Will send P.C. of Sphinx.

XXXXXX

Post-card.

This is the Sphinx. Goodness how Sad.

Post-card.

This is temple of someone. Darling I cant wait to tell you I'm engaged to Arthur. Arthur

47

is the one I thought was a pansy. Bertie
thinks egyptian art is v. inartistic.

Post-card.

This is Tutankhamens v. famous Tomb.
Bertie says it is vulgar and is engaged to
Miss P. so hes not one to speak and I call
her Mabel now. G how S. Bill wont speak
to Bertie Robert wont speak to me Papa and
Lady M. seem to have had a row there was a
man with a snake in a bag also a little boy
who told my fortune which was v. prosperous
Mum bought a shawl.

Post-card.

Saw this Mosque today. Robert is engaged
to a new girl called something or other who is
lousy.

S.S. *Glory of Greece*

Darling,
    Well so we all came back from Egypt pretty
excited and the cynical purser said what news
and I said *news* well Im engaged to Arthur

and Bertie is engaged to Miss P. and she is called Mabel now which is hardest of all to bear I said and Robert to a lousy girl and Papa has had a row with Lady M. and Bill has had a row with Bertie and Roberts lousy girl was awful to me and Arthur was sweet but the cynical purser wasnt a bit surprised on account he said people always get engaged and have quarrels on the Egyptian trip every cruise so I said I wasnt in the habit of getting engaged lightly thank you and he said I wasnt apparently in the habit of going to Egypt so I wont speak to him again nor will Arthur.

All love.

S.S. *Glory of Greece*

Sweet,

This is Algiers *not* very eastern in fact full of frogs. So it is all off with Arthur I was right about him at the first but who I am engaged to is Robert which is *much* better for all concerned really particularly Arthur on account of what I said originally first impressions always right. Yes ? No ? Robert and I drove about all day in the Botanic gardens and Goodness he was Decent. Bertie got plastered and had a row with Mabel—Miss P. again—so thats all right too and Robert's lousy girl spent all day on board with second officer. Mum bought shawl. Bill told Lady M. about his disillusionment and she told Robert who said yes we all know so Lady M. said it was very unreticent of Bill and she had very little respect for him and didnt blame his wife or the foreigner.

Love.

Post-card.

I forget what I said in my last letter but if I mentioned a lousy man called Robert you can take it as unsaid. This is still Algiers and Papa ate *dubious oysters* but is all right. Bertie went to a house full of tarts when he was plastered and is pretty unreticent about it as Lady M. would say.

Post-card.

So now we are back and sang old lang syne is that how you spell it and I kissed Arthur but wont speak to Robert and he cried not Robert I mean Arthur so then Bertie apologised to most of the people hed insulted but Miss P. walked away pretending not to hear. Goodness what a bitch.

PERIOD PIECE

LADY AMELIA had been educated in the belief that it was the height of impropriety to read a novel in the morning. Now, in the twilight of her days, when she had singularly little to occupy the two hours between her appearance downstairs at quarter past eleven, hatted and fragrant with lavender water, and the announcement of luncheon, she adhered rigidly to this principle. As soon as luncheon was over, however, and coffee had been served in the drawing room; before the hot milk in his saucer had sufficiently cooled for Manchu to drink it; while the sunlight, in summer, streamed through the Venetian blinds of the round-fronted Regency windows; while, in winter, the carefully stacked coal-fire glowed in its round-fronted grate; while Manchu sniffed and sipped at his saucer, and Lady Amelia spread out on her knees the various shades of coarse wool with which her failing eyesight now compelled her to work; while the elegant Regency clock ticked off the two and a half hours to tea time—it was Miss Myers' duty to read a novel aloud to her employer.

With the passing years Lady Amelia had grown increasingly fond of novels, and of novels of a particular type. They were what the assistant in the circulating library termed " strong meat " and kept in a hidden place under her desk. It was Miss Myers' duty to fetch and return them. "Have you anything of the kind Lady Amelia likes ? " she would ask sombrely.

" Well, there's this just come in," the assistant would answer, fishing up a volume from somewhere near her feet.

At one time Lady Amelia had enjoyed love stories about the irresponsible rich ; then she had had a psychological phase ; at the moment her interests were American, in the school of brutal realism and gross slang. " Something else like *Sanctuary* or *Bessie Cotter*," Miss Myers was reluctantly obliged to demand. And as the still afternoon was disturbed by her delicately modulated tones enunciating page by page, in scarcely comprehensible idiom, the narratives of rape and betrayal, Lady Amelia would occasionally chuckle a little over her woolwork.

"Women of my age always devote themselves either to religion or novels," she said. " I have remarked among my few surviving friends that those who read novels enjoy far better health."

The story they were reading came to an end at half-past four.

"Thank you," said Lady Amelia. "That was *most* entertaining. Make a note of the author's name, please, Miss Myers. You will be able to go to the library after tea and see whether they have another. I hope you enjoyed it."

"Well, it was very sad, wasn't it ? "

"Sad ? "

"I mean the poor young man who wrote it must come from a terrible home."

"Why do you say that, Miss Myers ? "

"Well, it was so far fetched."

"It is odd you should think so. I invariably find modern novels painfully reticent. Of course until lately I never read novels at all. I cannot say what they were like formerly. I was far too busy in the old days living my own life and sharing the lives of my friends— all people who came from anything but terrible homes," she added with a glance at her companion ; a glance sharp and smart as a rap on the knuckles with an ivory ruler.

There was half-an-hour before tea ; Manchu was asleep on the hearth rug, before the fireless grate ; the sun streamed in through the blinds, casting long strips of light on the Aubusson carpet. Lady Amelia fixed her eyes on the

embroidered, heraldic firescreen ; and proceeded dreamily. " I suppose it would not do.
You couldn't write about the things which
actually happen. People are so used to novels
that they would not believe them. The poor
writers are constantly at pains to make the
truth seem probable. Dear me, I often think,
as you sit, *so kindly*, reading to me, ' If one
was just to write down quite simply the events
of a few years in *any* household one knows . . .
No one would believe it.' I can hear you
yourself, dear Miss Myers, saying, ' Perhaps
these things *do* happen, very occasionally, once
in a century, in terrible homes ' ; instead of
which they are constantly happening, every
day, all round us—or at least, they were in my
young days.

" Take for example the extremely ironic
circumstances of the succession of the present
Lord Cornphillip :

" I used to know the Cornphillips very well
in the old days," said Lady Amelia—" Etty
was a cousin of my mother's—and when we
were first married my husband and I used to
stay there every autumn for the pheasant
shooting. Billy Cornphillip was a *very* dull
man—very dull indeed. He was in my
husband's regiment. I used to know a great
many dull people at the time when I was first

married, but Billy Cornphillip was notorious
for dullness even among my husband's friends.
Their place is in Wiltshire. I see the boy is
trying to sell it now. I am not surprised. It
was very ugly and very unhealthy. I used to
dread our visits there.

"Etty was entirely different, a lively little
thing with very nice eyes. People thought her
fast. Of course it was a *very* good match for
her; she was one of seven sisters and her
father was a younger son, poor dear. Billy
was twelve years older. She had been after
him for years. I remember crying with pleasure
when I received her letter telling me of the
engagement . . . It was at the breakfast
table . . . she used a very artistic kind of
writing paper with pale blue edges and bows
of blue ribbon at the corner . . .

"Poor Etty was always being artistic; she
tried to do something with the house—put up
peacocks' feathers and painted tambourines
and some very modern stencil work—but
the result was always depressing. She made a
little garden for herself at some distance from
the house, with a high wall and a padlocked
door, where she used to retire to think—or so
she said—for hours at a time. She called it
the Garden of Her Thoughts. I went in with
her once, as a great privilege, after one of her

quarrels with Billy. Nothing grew very well there—because of the high walls, I suppose, and her doing it all herself. There was a mossy seat in the middle. I suppose she used to sit on it while she thought. The whole place had a nasty dank smell . . .

"Well we were all delighted by Etty's luck and I think she quite liked Billy at first and was prepared to behave well to him, in spite of his dullness. You see it came just when we had all despaired. Billy had been the friend of Lady Instow for a long time and we were all afraid she would never let him marry but they had a quarrel at Cowes that year and Billy went up to Scotland in a bad temper and little Etty was staying in the house; so everything was arranged and I was one of her bridesmaids.

"The only person who was not pleased was Ralph Bland. You see he was Billy's nearest relative and would inherit if Billy died without children and he had got very hopeful as time went on.

"He came to a very sad end—in fact I don't know *what* became of him—but at the time of which I am speaking he was extremely popular, especially with women . . . Poor Viola Chasm was terribly in love with him. Wanted to run away. She and Lady Anchorage were very jealous of each other about him. It became quite disagreeable, particularly when Viola found that Lady Anchorage was paying her maid five pounds a week to send on all Ralph's letters to her—*before* Viola had read them, that was what she minded. He really had a most agreeable manner and said such ridiculous things . . . The marriage was a great disappointment to Ralph ; he was married himself and had two children. She had a little money at one time, but Ralph ran through it. Billy did not get on with Ralph—they had very little in common, of course—but he treated him quite well and was always getting him out of difficulties. In fact he made him a regular allowance at one time, and what with that and what he got from Viola and Lady Anchorage he was really quite comfortable. But, as he said, he had his children's future to consider, so that Billy's marriage *was* a *great* disappointment to him. He even talked of emigrating and Billy advanced him a large sum of money to purchase a sheep farm in New Zealand, but nothing came of that because Ralph had a Jewish friend in the city who made away with the entire amount. It all happened in a very unfortunate manner because Billy had given him this lump sum on the understanding that he should not expect an allowance. And then Viola and Lady Anchorage were greatly upset at his talk of leaving and made other arrangements so that in one way and another Ralph found himself in very low water, poor thing.

" However he began to recover his spirits when, after two years, there was no sign of an heir. People had babies very much more regularly when I was young. Everybody expected that Etty would have a baby—she was a nice healthy little thing—and when she did not, there was a great deal of ill natured gossip. Ralph himself behaved very wrongly in the matter. He used to make jokes about it, my husband told me, quite openly at his club in the worst possible taste.

" I well remember the last time that Ralph stayed with the Cornphillips ; it was a Christmas party and he came with his wife and his two children. The eldest boy was about six at the time and there was a very painful scene. I was not there myself, but we were staying nearby with the Lockejaws and of course we heard all about it. Billy seems to have been in his most pompous mood and was showing off the house when Ralph's little boy said solemnly and very loudly, ' Daddy says that when I step into your shoes I can pull the whole place down. The only thing worth worrying about is the money.'

" It was towards the end of a large and rather old-fashioned Christmas party, so no one was feeling in a forgiving mood. There was a final breach between the two cousins. Until then, in spite of the New Zealand venture, Billy had been reluctantly supporting Ralph. Now the allowance ceased once for all and Ralph took it in very bad part.

" You know what it is—or perhaps, dear Miss Myers, you are so fortunate as not to know what it is—when near relatives begin to quarrel. There is no limit to the savagery to which they will resort. I should be ashamed to indicate the behaviour of these two men towards each other during the next two or three years. No one had any sympathy with either.

" For example, Billy, of course, was a Conservative. Ralph came down and stood as a Radical in the General Election in his own county and got in.

" This, you must understand, was in the days before the lower classes began going into politics. It was customary for the candidates on both sides to be men of means and, in the circumstances, there was considerable expenditure involved. Much more in fact than Ralph could well afford, but in those days Members of Parliament had many opportunities for improving their position, so we all thought it a very wise course of Ralph's—the first really sensible thing we had known him do. What followed was *very* shocking.

" Billy of course had refused to lend his interest—that was only to be expected—but when the election was over, and everybody perfectly satisfied with the result, he did what I always consider a *Very Wrong Thing*. He made an accusation against Ralph of corrupt practices. It was a matter of three pounds which Ralph had given to a gardener whom Billy had discharged for drunkenness. I daresay that all that kind of thing has ceased nowadays, but at the time to which I refer, it was universally customary. No one had any sympathy with Billy but he pressed the charge and poor Ralph was unseated.

" Well, after this time, I really think that poor Ralph became a little unsettled in his mind. It is a very sad thing, Miss Myers, when a middle-aged man becomes obsessed by a grievance. You remember how difficult it was when the Vicar thought that Major Etheridge was persecuting him. He actually informed me that Major Etheridge put water in the petrol tank of his motor-cycle and gave

sixpences to the choir boys to sing out of tune
—well it was like that with poor Ralph. He
made up his mind that Billy had deliberately
ruined him. He took a cottage in the village
and used to embarrass Billy terribly by coming
to all the village fêtes and staring at Billy
fixedly. Poor Billy was always embarrassed
when he had to make a speech. Ralph used to
laugh ironically at the wrong places but never
so loudly that Billy could have him turned out.
And he used to go to public houses and drink
far too much. They found him asleep on the
terrace twice. And of course no one on the
place liked to offend him, because at any
moment he might become Lord Cornphillip.

" It must have been a very trying time for
Billy. He and Etty were not getting on at all
well together, poor things, and she spent more
and more time in the Garden of Her Thoughts
and brought out a very silly little book of
sonnets, mostly about Venice and Florence,
though she could never induce Billy to take
her abroad. He used to think that foreign
cooking upset him.

" Billy forbade her to speak to Ralph, which
was very awkward as they were always meeting
one another in the village and had been great
friends in the old days. In fact Ralph used
often to speak very contemptuously of his

cousin's manliness and say it was time someone took Etty off his hands. But that was only one of Ralph's jokes, because Etty had been getting terribly thin and dressing in the *most* artistic way, and Ralph *always* liked people who were chic and plump—like poor Viola Chasm. Whatever her faults——" said Lady Amelia, " Viola was always chic and plump.

" It was at the time of the Diamond Jubilee that the crisis took place. There was a bonfire and a great deal of merry making of a rather foolish kind and Ralph got terribly drunk. He began threatening Billy in a very silly way and Billy had him up before the magistrates and they made an order against him to keep the peace and not to reside within ten miles of Cornphillip. ' All right,' Ralph said, in front of the whole Court, ' I'll go away, but I won't go alone.' And will you believe it, Miss Myers, he and Etty went off to Venice together that very afternoon.

" Poor Etty, she had always wanted to go to Venice and had written so many poems about it, but it was a great surprise to us all. Apparently she had been meeting Ralph for some time in the Garden of Her Thoughts.

" I don't think Ralph ever cared about her,

because, as I say, she was not at all his type,
but it seemed to him a very good revenge on
Billy.

"Well, the elopement was far from successful.
They took rooms in a very insanitary palace,
and had a gondola and ran up a great many
bills.   Then Etty got a septic throat as a
result of the sanitation and while she was laid
up Ralph met an American woman who was
much more his type.   So in less than six weeks
poor Etty was back in England.   Of course
she did not go back to Billy at once.   She
wanted to stay with us, but, naturally, that
wasn't possible.   It was very awkward for
everyone.   There was never, I think, any
talk of a divorce.   It was long before that
became fashionable.   But we all felt it would
be very inconsiderate to Billy if we had her to
stay.   And then, this is what will surprise
you, Miss Myers, the next thing we heard was
that Etty was back at Cornphillip and about to
have a baby.   It was a son.   Billy was very
pleased about it and I don't believe that the
boy ever knew, until quite lately, at luncheon
with Lady Metroland, when my nephew Simon
told him, in a rather ill-natured way.

"As for poor Ralph's boy, I am afraid he has
come to very little good.   He must be middle
aged by now.   No one ever seems to hear

anything of him. Perhaps he was killed in war. I cannot remember.

" And here comes Ross with the tray ; and I see that Mrs. Samson has made more of those little scones which you always seem to enjoy so much. I am sure, dear Miss Myers, you would suffer much less from your *migraine* if you avoided them. But you take so little care of yourself, dear Miss Myers . . . Give one to Manchu."

ON GUARD

I

MILLICENT BLADE had a notable head of naturally fair hair; she had a docile and affectionate disposition, and an expression of face which changed with lightning rapidity from amiability to laughter and from laughter to respectful interest. But the feature which, more than any other, endeared her to sentimental Anglo-Saxon manhood was her nose.

It was not everybody's nose; many prefer one with greater body; it was not a nose to appeal to painters, for it was far too small and quite without shape, a mere dab of putty without apparent bone structure; a nose which made it impossible for its wearer to be haughty or imposing or astute. It would not have done for a governess or a 'cellist or even for a post office clerk, but it suited Miss Blade's book perfectly, for it was a nose that pierced the thin surface crust of the English heart to its warm and pulpy core; a nose to take the thoughts of English manhood back

69

to its schooldays, to the doughy-faced urchins on whom it had squandered its first affection, to memories of changing room and chapel and battered straw boaters. Three Englishmen in five, it is true, grow snobbish about these things in later life and prefer a nose that makes more show in public—but two in five is an average with which any girl of modest fortune may be reasonably content.

Hector kissed her reverently on the tip of this nose. As he did so, his senses reeled and in momentary delirium he saw the fading light of the November afternoon, the raw mist spreading over the playing fields ; overheated youth in the scrum ; frigid youth at the touch-line, shuffling on the duckboards, chafing their fingers and, when their mouths were emptied of biscuit crumbs, cheering their house team to further exertion.

"You will wait for me, won't you ? " he said.

"Yes, darling."

"And you will write ? "

"Yes, darling," she replied more doubtfully, "sometimes . . . at least I'll try. Writing is not my best thing, you know."

"I shall think of you all the time Out

There," said Hector. " It's going to be terrible—miles of impassable waggon track between me and the nearest white man, blinding sun, lions, mosquitoes, hostile natives, work from dawn until sunset singlehanded against the forces of nature, fever, cholera . . . But soon I shall be able to send for you to join me."

" Yes, darling."

" It's bound to be a success. I've discussed it all with Beckthorpe—that's the chap who's selling me the farm. You see the crop has failed every year so far—first coffee, then seisal, then tobacco, that's all you can grow there, and the year Beckthorpe grew seisal, everyone else was making a packet in tobacco, but seisal was no good ; then he grew tobacco, but by then it was coffee he ought to have grown, and so on. He stuck it nine years. Well if you work it out mathematically, Beckthorpe says, in three years one's bound to strike the right crop. I can't quite explain why but it is like roulette and all that sort of thing, you see."

" Yes, darling."

Hector gazed at her little, shapeless, mobile button of a nose and was lost again . . . " Play up, play up," and after the match the smell of crumpets being toasted over a gas-ring in his study . . .

2

Later that evening he dined with Beck-thorpe, and, as he dined, he grew more despondent.

" Tomorrow this time I shall be at sea," he said, twiddling his empty port glass.

" Cheer up, old boy," said Beckthorpe.

Hector filled his glass and gazed with growing distaste round the reeking dining room of Beckthorpe's club. The last awful member had left the room and they were alone with the cold buffet.

" I say, you know, I've been trying to work it out. It *was* in three years you said the crop was bound to be right, wasn't it ? "

" That's right, old boy."

" Well, I've been through the sum and it seems to me that it may be eighty-one years before it comes right."

" No, no, old boy, three or nine or at the most twenty-seven."

" Are you sure ? "

" Quite."

" Good . . . you know it's awful leaving Milly behind. Suppose it *is* eighty-one years before the crop succeeds. It's the devil of a time to expect a girl to wait. Some other blighter might turn up, if you see what I mean."

"In the Middle Ages they used to use girdles of chastity."

"Yes, I know. I've been thinking of them. But they sound damned uncomfortable. I doubt if Milly would wear one even if I knew where to find it."

"Tell you what, old boy. You ought to give her something."

"Hell, I'm always giving her things. She either breaks them or loses them or forgets where she got them."

"You must give her something she will always have by her, something that will last."

"Eighty-one years?"

"Well, say, twenty-seven. Something to remind her of you."

"I could give her a photograph—but I might change a bit in twenty-seven years."

"No, no, that would be most unsuitable. A photograph wouldn't do at all. I know what I'd give her. I'd give her a dog."

"Dog?"

"A healthy puppy that was over distemper and looked like living a long time. She might even call it Hector."

"Would that be a good thing, Beckthorpe?"

"Best possible, old boy."

So next morning, before catching the boat train, Hector hurried to one of the mammoth stores of London and was shown to the live-stock department. " I want a puppy."

" Yes, sir, any particular sort ? "

" One that will live a long time. Eighty-one years, or twenty-seven at the least."

The man looked doubtful. " We have some fine healthy puppies of course," he admitted, " but none of them carry a guarantee. Now if it was longevity you wanted, might I recommend a tortoise ? They live to an extraordinary age and are very safe in traffic."

" No, it must be a pup."

" Or a parrot ? "

" No, no, a pup. I would prefer one named Hector."

They walked together past monkeys and kittens and cockatoos to the dog department which, even at this early hour, had attracted a small congregation of rapt worshippers. There were puppies of all varieties in wire fronted kennels, ears cocked, tails wagging, noisily soliciting attention. Rather wildly, Hector selected a poodle and, as the salesman disappeared to fetch him his change, he leant down for a moment's intense communion with the beast of his choice. He gazed deep into the sharp little face, avoided a sudden snap and said with profound solemnity

" You are to look after Milly, Hector.

74

See that she doesn't marry anyone until I get back."

And the pup Hector waved his plume of tail.

3

Millicent came to see him off, but, negligently, went to the wrong station; it could not have mattered, however, for she was twenty minutes late. Hector and the poodle hung about the barrier looking for her, and not until the train was already moving did he bundle the animal into Beckthorpe's arms with instructions to deliver him at Millicent's address. Luggage labelled for Mombasa, " Wanted on the voyage," lay in the rack above him. He felt very much neglected.

That evening as the ship pitched and rolled past the Channel lighthouses, he received a radiogram : *Miserable to miss you went Paddington like idiot thank you thank you for sweet dog I love him father minds dreadfully longing to hear about farm dont fall for ship siren all love Milly.*

In the Red Sea he received another. *Beware sirens puppy bit man called Mike.*

After that Hector heard nothing of Millicent except for a Christmas card which arrived in the last days of February.

75

4

Generally speaking, Millicent's fancy for any particular young man was likely to last four months. It depended on how far he had got in that time whether the process of extinction was sudden or protracted. In the case of Hector, her affection had been due to diminish at about the time that she became engaged to him; it had been artificially prolonged during the succeeding three weeks, during which he made strenuous, infectiously earnest efforts to find employment in England; it came to an abrupt end with his departure for Kenya. Acccrdingly the duties of the puppy Hector began with his first days at home. He was young for the job and wholly inexperienced; it is impossible to blame him for his mistake in the matter of Mike Boswell.

This was a young man who had enjoyed a wholly unromantic friendship with Millicent since she first came out. He had seen her fair hair in all kinds of light, in and out of doors, crowned in hats in succeeding fashions, bound with ribbon, decorated with combs, jauntily stuck with flowers; he had seen her nose uplifted in all kinds of weather, had even, on occasions, playfully tweaked it with his finger and thumb, and had never for one moment felt remotely attracted by her.

But the puppy Hector could hardly be expected to know this. All he knew was that two days after receiving his commission, he observed a tall and personable man of marriageable age who treated his hostess with the sort of familiarity which, among the kennel maids with whom he had been brought up, meant only one thing.

The two young people were having tea together. Hector watched for some time from his place on the sofa, barely stifling his growls. A climax was reached when, in the course of some barely intelligible back-chat, Mike leant forward and patted Millicent on the knee.

It was not a serious bite, a mere snap, in fact ; but Hector had small teeth as sharp as pins. It was the sudden, nervous speed with which Mike withdrew his hand which caused the damage ; he swore, wrapped his hand in a handkerchief, and at Millicent's entreaty revealed three or four minute wounds. Millicent spoke harshly to Hector and tenderly to Mike, and hurried to her mother's medicine cupboard for a bottle of iodine.

Now no Englishman, however phlegmatic, can have his hand dabbed with iodine without, momentarily at any rate, falling in love.

Mike had seen the nose countless times before, but that afternoon, as it was bowed over his scratched thumb, and as Millicent said, " Am I hurting terribly ? ", as it was raised towards him, and as Millicent said, " There. Now it will be all right," Mike suddenly saw it transfigured as its devotees saw it and from that moment, until long after the three months of attention which she accorded him, he was Millicent's besotted suitor.

The pup Hector saw all this and realised his mistake. Never again, he decided, would he give Millicent the excuse to run for the iodine bottle.

5

He had on the whole an easy task, for Millicent's naturally capricious nature could, as a rule, be relied upon, unaided, to drive her lovers into extremes of irritation. Moreover she had come to love the dog. She received very regular letters from Hector, written weekly and arriving in batches of three or four according to the mails. She always opened them ; often she read them to the end, but their contents made little impression upon her mind and gradually their writer drifted into oblivion so that when people said to her " How is darling Hector ? " it came naturally to her to reply, " He doesn't like the hot weather much I'm afraid, and his coat is in a very poor state. I'm thinking of having him plucked," instead of, " He had a go of malaria and there is black worm in his tobacco crop."

Playing upon this affection which had grown up for him, Hector achieved a technique for dealing with Millicent's young men. He no longer growled at them or soiled their trousers ; that merely resulted in his being turned from the room ; instead, he found it increasingly easy to usurp the conversation.

Tea was the most dangerous time of day, for then Millicent was permitted to entertain friends in her sitting-room ; accordingly, though he had a constitutional preference for pungent, meaty dishes, Hector heroically simulated a love of lump sugar. Having made this apparent, at whatever cost to his digestion, it was easy to lead Millicent on to an interest in tricks ; he would beg and " trust," lie down as though dead, stand in the corner and raise a fore paw to his ear.

" What does S U G A R spell ? " Millicent would ask and Hector would walk round the tea table to the sugar-bowl and lay his nose against it, gazing earnestly and clouding the silver with his moist breath.

" He understands everything," Millicent would say in triumph.

When tricks failed Hector would demand to be let out of the door. The young man would be obliged to interrupt himself to open it. Once on the other side Hector would scratch and whine for re-admission.

In moments of extreme anxiety Hector would affect to be sick—no difficult feat after the unwelcome diet of lump sugar ; he would stretch out his neck, retching noisily, till Millicent snatched him up and carried him to the hall, where the floor, paved in marble, was less vulnerable—but by that time a tender atmosphere had been shattered and one wholly prejudicial to romance created to take its place.

This series of devices spaced out through the afternoon and tactfully obtruded whenever the guest showed signs of leading the conversation to a more intimate phase, distracted young man after young man and sent them finally away, baffled and despairing.

Every morning Hector lay on Millicent's bed while she took her breakfast and read the daily paper. This hour from ten to eleven was sacred to the telephone and it was then that the young men with whom she had danced overnight attempted to renew their friendship and make plans for the day. At first Hector sought, not unsuccessfully, to prevent these assignations by entangling himself in the wire, but soon a subtler and more insulting technique suggested itself. He pretended to telephone too. Thus, as soon as the bell rang, he would wag his tail and cock his head on one side in a way that he had learned was engaging. Millicent would begin her conversation and Hector would wriggle up under her arm and nuzzle against the receiver.

"Listen," she would say, "*someone* wants to talk to you. Isn't he an angel?" Then she would hold the receiver down to him and the young man at the other end would be dazed by a shattering series of yelps. This accomplishment appealed so much to Millicent that often she would not even bother to find out the name of the caller but, instead, would take off the receiver and hold it directly to the black snout, so that some wretched young man half a mile away, feeling, perhaps, none too well in the early morning, found himself barked to silence before he had spoken a word.

At other times young men badly taken with the nose, would attempt to waylay Millicent in Hyde Park when she was taking Hector for exercise. Here, at first, Hector would get lost, fight other dogs and bite small children to keep himself constantly in her attention, but soon he adopted a gentler course. He insisted upon carrying Millicent's bag for her. He would trot in front of the couple and whenever he thought an interruption desirable he would drop the bag; the young man was obliged to pick it up and restore it first to Millicent and then, at her request, to the dog. Few young men were sufficiently servile to submit to more than one walk in these degrading conditions.

In this way two years passed. Letters arrived constantly from Kenya, full of devotion, full of minor disasters—blight in the seisal, locusts in the coffee, labour troubles, drought, flood, the local government, the world market. Occasionally Millicent read the letters aloud to the dog, usually she left them unread on her breakfast tray. She and Hector moved together through the leisurely routine of English social life. Wherever she carried her nose, two in five marriageable men fell temporarily in love; wherever Hector followed their ardour changed to irritation, shame and disgust. Mothers began to remark complacently that it was curious how that fascinating Blade girl never got married.

6

At last in the third year of this régime a new problem presented itself in the person of Major Sir·Alexander Dreadnought, Bart., M.P., and Hector immediately realised that he was up against something altogether more formidable than he had hitherto tackled.

Sir Alexander was not a young man ; he was forty-five and a widower. He was wealthy, popular and preternaturally patient ; he was also mildly distinguished, being joint-master of a Midland pack of hounds and a junior Minister ; he bore a war record of conspicuous gallantry. Millie's father and mother were delighted when they saw that her nose was having its effect on him. Hector took against him from the first, exerted every art which his two and a half years' practice had perfected, and achieved nothing. Devices that had driven a dozen young men to frenzies of chagrin seemed only to accentuate Sir Alexander's tender solicitude. When he came to the house to fetch Millicent for the evening he was found to have filled the pockets of his evening clothes with lump sugar for Hector ; when Hector was sick Sir Alexander was there first, on his knees with a page of *The Times ;* Hector resorted to his early, violent manner and bit

83

him frequently and hard, but Sir Alexander merely remarked, " I believe I am making the little fellow jealous. A delightful trait."

For the truth was that Sir Alexander had been persecuted long and bitterly from his earliest days—his parents, his sisters, his schoolfellows, his company-sergeant and his colonel, his colleagues in politics, his wife, his joint-master, huntsman and hunt secretary, his election agent, his constituents and even his parliamentary private secretary had one and all pitched into Sir Alexander, and he accepted this treatment as a matter of course. For him it was the most natural thing in the world to have his eardrums outraged by barks when he rang up the young woman of his affections; it was a high privilege to retrieve her handbag when Hector dropped it in the Park; the small wounds that Hector was able to inflict on his ankles and wrists were to him knightly scars. In his more ambitious moments he referred to Hector in Millicent's hearing as " my little rival ". There could be no doubt whatever of his intentions and when he asked Millicent and her mama to visit him in the country, he added at the foot of the letter, " *Of course the invitation includes little Hector.*"

The Saturday to Monday visit to Sir Alexander's was a nightmare to the poodle. He worked as he had never worked before ; every artifice by which he could render his presence odious was attempted and attempted in vain. As far as his host was concerned, that is to say. The rest of the household responded well enough, and he received a vicious kick when, through his own bad management, he found himself alone with the second footman, whom he had succeeded in upsetting with a tray of cups at tea time.

Conduct that had driven Millicent in shame from half the stately homes of England was meekly accepted here. There were other dogs in the house—elderly, sober, well-behaved animals at whom Hector flew ; they turned their heads sadly away from his yaps of defiance, he snapped at their ears. They lolloped sombrely out of reach and Sir Alexander had them shut away for the rest of the visit.

There was an exciting Aubusson carpet in the dining-room to which Hector was able to do irreparable damage ; Sir Alexander seemed not to notice.

Hector found a carrion in the park and conscientiously rolled in it—although such a thing was obnoxious to his nature—and, returning, fouled every chair in the drawing-room; Sir Alexander himself helped Millicent wash him and brought some bath salts from his own bathroom for the operation.

Hector howled all night; he hid and had half the household searching for him with lanterns; he killed some young pheasants and made a sporting attempt on a peacock. All to no purpose. He staved off an actual proposal, it is true—once in the Dutch garden, once on the way to the stables and once while he was being bathed—but when Monday morning arrived and he heard Sir Alexander say, " I hope Hector enjoyed his visit a little. I hope I shall see him here *very, very* often," he knew that he was defeated.

It was now only a matter of waiting. The evenings in London were a time when it was impossible for him to keep Millicent under observation. One of these days he would wake up to hear Millicent telephoning to her girl friends, breaking the good news of her engagement.

Thus it was that after a long conflict of loyalties he came to a desperate resolve. He had grown fond of his young mistress; often and often when her face had been pressed down to his he had felt sympathy with that long line of young men whom it was his duty to persecute. But Hector was no kitchen-haunting mongrel. By the code of all well-born dogs it is money that counts. It is the purchaser, not the mere feeder and fondler, to whom ultimate loyalty is due. The hand which had once fumbled with the fivers in the live-stock department of the mammoth store, now tilled the unfertile soil of equatorial Africa, but the sacred words of commission still rang in Hector's memory. All through the Sunday night and the journey of Monday morning, Hector wrestled with his problem ; then he came to the decision. *The nose must go.*

7

It was an easy business ; one firm snap as she bent over his basket and the work was accomplished. She went to a plastic surgeon and emerged some weeks later without scar or stitch. But it was a different nose ; the surgeon in his way was an artist and, as I have said above, Millicent's nose had no sculptural qualities. Now she has a fine aristocratic beak, worthy of the spinster she is about to become. Like all spinsters she watches eagerly for the

foreign mails and keeps carefully under lock
and key a casket full of depressing agricul-
tural intelligence ; like all spinsters she is
accompanied everywhere by an ageing lap-
dog.

INCIDENT IN AZANIA

Azania is a large, imaginary island off the East Coast of Africa; in character and history a combination of Zanzibar and Abyssinia. At the end of Black Mischief *the native administration was overthrown and a joint protectorate established by the British and French.* Several of the characters in this story appeared in Black Mischief.

I

THE UNION CLUB at Matodi was in
marked contrast to the hillside, bungalow
dwellings of the majority of its members.
It stood in the centre of the town, on the water
front; a seventeenth-century Arab mansion
built of massive whitewashed walls round a
small court; latticed windows overhung the
street from which, in former times, the women-
folk of a great merchant had watched the passing
traffic; a heavy door, studded with brass bosses
gave entrance to the dark shade of the court,
where a little fountain sprayed from the roots
of an enormous mango; and an open staircase of inlaid cedar-wood led to the cool
interior.

An Arab porter, clothed in a white gown
scoured and starched like a Bishop's surplice,
crimson sash and tarboosh, sat drowsily at the
gate. He rose in reverence as Mr. Reppington,
the magistrate, and Mr. Bretherton, the
sanitary-inspector, proceeded splendidly to the
bar.

In token of the cordiality of the Condominium, French officials were honorary members of the Club, and a photograph of a former French President (" We can't keep changing it," said Major Lepperidge, " every time the frogs care to have a shimozzle ") hung in the smoking room opposite the portrait of the Prince of Wales; except on Gala nights, however, they rarely availed themselves of their privilege. The single French journal to which the Club subscribed was *La Vie Parisienne*, which, on this particular evening, was in the hands of a small man of plebeian appearance, sitting alone in a basket chair.

Reppington and Bretherton nodded their way forward. " Evening, Granger." " Evening, Barker." " Evening, Jagger," and then in an audible undertone Bretherton inquired, " Who's the chap in the corner with *La Vie ?* "

" Name of Brooks. Petrol or something."

" Ah."

" Pink Gin ? "

" Ah."

" What sort of day ? "

" Bad show, rather. Trouble about draining the cricket field. No subsoil."

" Ah. Bad show."

The Goan barman put their drinks before them.   Bretherton signed the chit.

" Well, cheerioh."

" Cheerioh."

Mr. Brooks remained riveted upon *La Vie Parisienne*.

Presently Major Lepperidge came in, and the atmosphere stiffened a little.   (He was O.C. of the native levy, seconded from India.)

" Evening, Major," from civilians.   " Good evening, sir," from the military.

" Evening.   Evening.   Evening.   Phew. Just had a very fast set of lawner with young Kentish.   Hot service.   Gin and lime.   By the way, Bretherton, the cricket field is looking pretty seedy."

" I know.   No subsoil."

" I say, that's a bad show.   *No subsoil.*   Well, do what you can, there's a good fellow.   It looks terrible.   Quite bare and a great lake in the middle."

The Major took his gin and lime and moved towards a chair ; suddenly he saw Mr. Brooks, and his authoritative air softened to unaccustomed amiability.   " Why, hallo, Brooks," he said.   " How are you ?   Fine to see you back. Just had the pleasure of seeing your daughter at the tennis club.   My missus wondered if you and she would care to come up and dine one

93

evening. How about Thursday? Grand.
She'll be delighted. Good-night you fellows.
Got to get a shower."

The occurrence was sensational. Bretherton
and Reppington looked at one another in
shocked surprise.

Major Lepperidge, both in rank and
personality, was the leading man in Matodi—
in the whole of Azania indeed, with the single
exception of the Chief Commissioner at Debra
Dowa. It was inconceivable that Brooks
should dine with Lepperidge. Bretherton
himself had only dined there once and *he* was
Government.

" Hullo, Brooks," said Reppington
" Didn't see you there behind your paper.
Come and have one."

" Yes, Brooks," said Bretherton. " Didn't
know you were back. Have a jolly leave?
See any shows? "

" It's very kind of you, but I must be going.
We arrived on Tuesday in the *Ngoma*. No, I
didn't see any shows. You see, I was down at
Bournemouth most of the time."

" One before you go."

" No really, thanks, I must get back. My
daughter will be waiting. Thanks all the same
See you both later."

Daughter . . . ?

2

There were eight Englishwomen in Matodi, counting Mrs. Bretherton's two-year-old daughter; nine if you included Mrs. Macdonald (but no one *did* include Mrs. Macdonald who came from Bombay and betrayed symptoms of Asiatic blood. Besides, no one knew who Mr. Macdonald had been. Mrs. Macdonald kept an ill-frequented *pension* on the outskirts of the town named " The Bougainvillea "). All who were of marriageable age were married; they led lives under a mutual scrutiny too close and unremitting for romance. There were, however, seven unmarried Englishmen, three in Government service, three in commerce and one unemployed, who had fled to Matodi from his creditors in Kenya. (He sometimes spoke vaguely of " planting " or " prospecting ", but in the meantime drew a small remittance each month and hung amiably about the Club and the tennis courts.)

Most of these bachelors were understood to have some girl at home; they kept photographs in their rooms, wrote long letters regularly, and took their leave with hints that when they returned they might not be alone. But they invariably were. Perhaps in precipitous eagerness for sympathy they painted too dark a

95

picture of Azanian life; perhaps the Tropics made them a little addle-pated. . . .

Anyway, the arrival of Prunella Brooks sent a wave of excitement through English society. Normally, as the daughter of Mr. Brooks, oil company agent, her choice would have been properly confined to the three commercial men—Mr. James, of the Eastern Exchange Telegraph Company, and Messrs. Watson and Jagger, of the Bank—but Prunella was a girl of such evident personal superiority, that in her first afternoon at the tennis courts, as has been shown above, she transgressed the shadow line effortlessly and indeed unconsciously, and stepped straight into the inmost sanctuary, the Lepperidge bungalow.

She was small and unaffected, an iridescent blonde, with a fresh skin, doubly intoxicating in contrast with the tanned and desiccated tropical complexions around her; with rubbery, puppyish limbs and a face which lit up with amusement at the most barren pleasantries; an air of earnest interest in the opinions and experiences of all she met; a natural *confidante*, with no disposition to make herself the centre of a group, but rather to tackle her friends one by one, in their own time, when they needed her; deferential and charming to the married women; tender, friendly,

96

and mildly flirtatious with the men; keen on
games but not so good as to shake masculine
superiority; a devoted daughter denying herself any pleasure that might impair the smooth
working of Mr. Brooks's home—" No, I
must go now. I couldn't let father come home
from the Club and not find me there to greet
him "—in fact, just such a girl as would be a
light and blessing in any outpost of the Empire.
It was very few days before all at Matodi were
eloquent of their good fortune.

Of course, she had first of all to be examined
and instructed by the matrons of the colony,
but she submitted to her initiation with so
pretty a grace that she might not have been
aware of the dangers of the ordeal. Mrs.
Lepperidge and Mrs. Reppington put her
through it. Far away in the interior, in the
sunless secret places, where a twisted stem
across the jungle track, a rag fluttering to the
bough of a tree, a fowl headless and full spread
by an old stump marked the taboo where no
man might cross, the Sakuya women chanted
their primeval litany of initiation; here on the
hillside the no less terrible ceremony was held
over Mrs. Lepperidge's tea table. First the
questions; disguised and delicate over the tea
cake but quickening their pace as the tribal
rhythm waxed high and the table was cleared

97

of tray and kettle, falling faster and faster like
ecstatic hands on the taut cow-hide, mounting
and swelling with the first cigarette ; a series
of urgent, peremptory interrogations. To all
this Prunella responded with docile simplicity.
The whole of her life, upbringing and education were exposed, examined and found to be
exemplary ; her mother's death, the care of an
aunt, a convent school in the suburbs which
had left her with charming manners, a readiness
to find the right man and to settle down with
him whenever the Service should require it ;
her belief in a limited family and European
education, the value of sport, kindness to
animals, affectionate patronage of men.

Then, when she had proved herself worthy
of it, came the instruction. Intimate details of
health and hygiene, things every young girl
should know, the general dangers of sex and
its particular dangers in the Tropics ; the
proper treatment of the other inhabitants of
Matodi, etiquette towards ladies of higher
rank, the leaving of cards. . . . "*Never* shake
hands with natives, however well educated they
think themselves. Arabs are quite different,
many of them very like gentlemen . . . no
worse than a great many Italians, really . . .
Indians, luckily, you won't have to meet . . .
never allow native servants to see you in your

dressing gown . . . and be *very* careful about curtains in the bathroom—*natives peep* . . . never walk in the side streets alone—in fact you have no business in them at all . . . never ride outside the compound alone. There have been several cases of bandits . . . an American missionary only last year, but he was some kind of non-Conformist . . . *We owe it to our men folk* to take no unnecessary risks . . . a band of brigands commanded by a Sakuya called Joab . . . the Major will soon clean him up when he gets the levy into better shape . . . they find their boots very uncomfortable at present[1] . . . meanwhile it is a very safe rule to take a *man* with you *everywhere*. . . . "

3

And Prunella was never short of male escort. As the weeks passed it became clear to the watching colony that her choice had narrowed down to two—Mr. Kentish, assistant native commissioner, and Mr. Benson, second lieutenant in the native levy ; not that she was not consistently charming to everyone else— even to the shady remittance man and the repulsive Mr. Jagger—but by various little

[1] See *Black Mischief.*

acts of preference she made it known that
Kentish and Benson were her favourites. And
the study of their innocent romances gave a
sudden new interest to the social life of the
town. Until now there had been plenty of
entertaining certainly—gymkhanas and tennis
tournaments, dances and dinner parties, calling
and gossiping, amateur opera and church
bazaars—but it had been a joyless and dutiful
affair. They knew what was expected of
Englishmen abroad; they had to keep up
appearances before the natives and their co-
protectionists; they had to have something to
write home about; so they sturdily went
through the recurring recreations due to their
station. But with Prunella's coming a new
lightness was in the air; there were more
parties and more dances and a point to everything. Mr. Brooks, who had never dined out
before, found himself suddenly popular, and as
his former exclusion had not worried him, he
took his present vogue as a natural result of his
daughter's charm, was pleased by it and mildly
embarrassed. He realised that she would soon
want to get married and faced with equanimity
the prospect of his inevitable return to solitude.

Meanwhile Benson and Kentish ran neck
and neck through the crowded Azanian spring
and no one could say with confidence which

was leading—betting was slightly in favour of Benson, who had supper dances with her at the Caledonian and the Polo Club Balls—when there occurred the incident which shocked Azanian feeling to its core. Prunella Brooks was kidnapped.

The circumstances were obscure and a little shady. Prunella, who had never been known to infringe one jot or tittle of the local code, had been out riding alone in the hills. That was apparent from the first, and later, under cross-examination, her syce revealed that this had for some time been her practice, two or three times a week. The shock of her infidelity to rule was almost as great as the shock of her disappearance.

But worse was to follow. One evening at the Club, since Mr. Brooks was absent (his popularity had waned in the last few days and his presence made a painful restraint) the question of Prunella's secret rides was being freely debated, when a slightly fuddled voice broke into the conversation.

" It's bound to come out," said the remittance man from Kenya, " so I may as well tell you right away. Prunella used to ride with *me*. She didn't want us to get talked about, so we met on the Debra Dowa road by the Moslem Tombs. I shall miss those afternoons very much indeed," said the remittance man, a slight, alcoholic quaver in his voice, " and I blame myself to a great extent for all that has happened. You see, I must have had a little more to drink than was good for me that morning and it was very hot, so with one thing and another, when I went to change into riding breeches I fell asleep and did not wake up until after dinner time. And perhaps that is the last we shall ever see of her . . . " and two vast tears rolled down his cheeks.

This unmanly spectacle preserved the peace, for Benson and Kentish had already begun to advance upon the remittance man with a menacing air. But there is little satisfaction in castigating one who is already in the profound depths of self-pity and the stern tones of Major Lepperidge called them sharply to order. " Benson, Kentish, I don't say I don't sympathise with you boys and I know exactly what I'd do myself under the circumstances. The story we have just heard may or may not be the truth. In either case I think I know what we all feel about the teller. But that can wait. You'll have plenty of time to settle up when we've got Miss Brooks safe. That is our first duty."

Thus exhorted, public opinion again rallied to Prunella, and the urgency of her case was dramatically emphasised two days later by the arrival at the American Consulate of the Baptist missionary's right ear loosely done up in newspaper and string. The men of the colony—excluding, of course, the remittance man—got together in the Lepperidge bungalow and formed a committee of defence, first to protect the women who were still left to them and then to rescue Miss Brooks at whatever personal inconvenience or risk.

4

The first demand for ransom came through the agency of Mr. Youkoumian. The little Armenian was already well known and, on the whole, well liked by the English community; it did them good to find a foreigner who so completely fulfilled their ideal of all that a foreigner should be. Two days after the foundation of the British Womanhood Protection Committee, he appeared at the major's orderly room asking for a private audience, a cheerful, rotund, self-abasing figure, in a shiny alpaca suit, skull cap and yellow, elastic-sided boots.

" Major Lepperidge," he said, " you know me; all the gentlemen in Matodi know me.

The English are my favourite gentlemen and
the natural protectors of the under races all
same as the League of Nations. Listen, Major
Lepperidge, I ear things. Everyone trusts me.
It is a no good thing for these black men to
abduct English ladies. I fix it O.K."

To the Major's questions, with infinite
evasions and circumlocutions, Youkoumian
explained that by the agency of various cousins
of his wife he had formed contact with an
Arab, one of whose wives was the sister of a
Sakuya in Joab's band ; that Miss Brooks was
at present safe and that Joab was disposed to
talk business. "Joab make very stiff price,"
he said. "He want one undred thousand
dollars, an armoured car, two machine guns,
a undred rifles, five thousand rounds of ammuni-
tion, fifty orses, fifty gold wrist watches, a
wireless set, fifty cases of whisky, free pardon
and the rank of honorary colonel in the Azanian
levy."

"That, of course, is out of the question."

The little Armenian shrugged his shoulders.
"Oh, well, then he cut off Miss Brooks' ears
all same as the American clergyman. Listen,
Major, this is one damn awful no good country.
I live ere forty years, I know. I been little man
and I been big man in this country, all same
rule for big and little. If native want anything

you give it im quick, then work ell out of im and get it back later. Natives all damn fool men but very savage all same as animals. Listen, Major, I make best whisky in Matodi—Scotch, Irish, all brands I make im; I got very fine watches in my shop all same as gold, I got wireless set,—armoured car, orses, machine guns is for you to do. Then we clean up tidy bit fifty-fifty, no ? "

5

Two days later Mr. Youkoumian appeared at Mr. Brooks's bungalow. " A letter from Miss Brooks," he said. " A Sakuya fellow brought it in. I give im a rupee."

It was an untidy scrawl on the back of an envelope.

Dearest Dad,

I am safe at present and fairly well. On no account attempt to follow the messenger. Joab and the bandits would torture me to death. Please send gramophone and records. Do come to terms or I don't know what will happen.

Prunella.

It was the first of a series of notes which, from now on, arrived every two or three days through the agency of Mr. Youkoumian. They mostly contained requests for small personal possessions . . .

Dearest Dad,
Not those records. The dance ones. . . . Please send face cream in pot in bathroom, also illustrated papers . . . the green silk pyjamas . . . Lucky Strike cigarettes . . . two light drill skirts and the sleeveless silk shirts . . .

The letters were all brought to the Club and read aloud, and as the days passed the sense of tension became less acute, giving way to a general feeling that the drama had become prosaic.

"They are bound to reduce their price. Meanwhile the girl is safe enough," pronounced Major Lepperidge, voicing authoritatively what had long been unspoken in the minds of the community.

The life of the town began to resume its normal aspect—administration, athletics, gossip; the American missionary's second ear arrived and attracted little notice, except from Mr. Youkoumian, who produced an ear trumpet which he attempted to sell to the mission headquarters. The ladies of the colony abandoned the cloistered life which they had adopted during the first scare; the

106

men became less protective and stayed out late at the Club as heretofore.

Then something happened to revive interest in the captive. Sam Stebbing discovered the cypher.

He was a delicate young man of high academic distinction, lately arrived from Cambridge to work with Grainger in the immigration office. From the first he had shown a keener interest than most of his colleagues in the situation. For a fortnight of oppressive heat he had sat up late studying the texts of Prunella's messages; then he emerged with the startling assertion that there was a cypher. The system by which he had solved it was far from simple. He was ready enough to explain it, but his hearers invariably lost hold of the argument and contented themselves with the solution.

". . . you see you translate it into Latin, you make an anagram of the first and last words of the first message, the second and last but one of the third when you start counting from the centre onwards. I bet that puzzled the bandits . . ."

" Yes, old boy. Besides, none of them can read anyway . . ."

" Then in the fourth message you go back to the original system, taking the fourth word and the last but three . . ."

" Yes, yes, I see. Don't bother to explain any more. Just tell us what the message really says."

" It says, 'DAILY THREATENED WORSE THAN BREATH.'

" Her system's at fault there, must mean ' death '; then there's a word I can't understand—PLZGF, no doubt the poor child was in great agitation when she wrote it, and after that TRUST IN MY KING."

This was generally voted a triumph. The husbands brought back the news to their wives.

" . . . Jolly ingenious the way old Stebbing worked it out. I won't bother to explain it to you. You wouldn't understand. Anyway, the result is clear enough. Miss Brooks is in terrible danger. We must all do something."

" But who would have thought of little Prunella being so clever . . ."

" Ah, I always said that girl had brains."

6

News of the discovery was circulated by the Press agencies throughout the civilised world. At first the affair had received wide attention. It had been front page, with portrait, for two days, then middle page with portrait, then middle page half way down without portrait, and finally page three of the *Excess* as the story became daily less alarming. The cypher gave the story a new lease of life. Stebbing, with portrait, appeared on the front page. Ten thousand pounds was offered by the paper towards the ransom, and a star journalist appeared from the skies in an aeroplane to conduct and report the negotiations.

He was a tough young man of Australian origin and from the moment of his arrival everything went with a swing. The colony sunk its habitual hostility to the Press, elected him to the Club, and filled his leisure with cocktail parties and tennis tournaments. He even usurped Lepperidge's position as authority on world topics.

But his stay was brief. On the first day he interviewed Mr. Brooks and everyone of importance in the town, and cabled back a moving " human " story of Prunella's position in the heart of the colony. From now onwards to three millions or so of readers Miss Brooks became Prunella. (There was only one local celebrity whom he was unable to meet. Poor Mr. Stebbing had " gone under " with the heat and had been shipped back to England on sick leave in a highly deranged condition of nerves and mind.)

On the second day he interviewed Mr. Youkoumian. They sat down together with a bottle of mastika at a little round table behind Mr. Youkoumian's counter at ten in the morning. It was three in the afternoon before the reporter stepped out into the white-dust heat, but he had won his way. Mr. Youkoumian had promised to conduct him to the bandits' camp. Both of them were pledged to secrecy. By sundown the whole of Matodi was discussing the coming expedition, but the journalist was not embarrassed by any inquiries; he was alone that evening, typing out an account of what he expected would happen next day.

He described the start at dawn . . . " grey light breaking over the bereaved township of Matodi . . . the camels snorting and straining at their reins . . . the many sorrowing Englishmen to whom the sun meant only the termination of one more night of hopeless watching . . . silver dawn breaking in the little room where Prunella's bed stood, the coverlet turned down as she had left it on the fatal afternoon . . ." He described the ascent into the hills——" . . . luxuriant tropical vegetation giving place to barren scrub and bare rock . . ." He described how the bandits' messenger blindfolded him and how he rode, swaying on his camel through darkness, into the unknown. Then, after what seemed an eternity, the halt; the bandage removed from his eyes . . . the bandits' camp. " . . . twenty pairs of remorseless eastern eyes glinting behind ugly-looking rifles . . ." here he took the paper from his machine and made a correction; the bandits' lair was to be in a cave " . . . littered with bone and skins." . . . Joab, the bandit chief, squatting in barbaric splendour, a jewelled sword across his knees. Then the climax of the story; Prunella bound. For some time he toyed with the idea of stripping her, and began to hammer out a vivid word-picture of her girlish frame shrinking in the shadows, Andromeda-like. But caution restrained him and he contented himself with " . . . her lovely, slim body marked by the hempen ropes that cut into her young limbs . . ." The concluding paragraphs related how despair suddenly melted to hope in her eyes as he stepped forward, handing over the ransom to the bandit chief and " in the name of the *Daily Excess* and the People of Great Britain restored her to her heritage of freedom."

It was late before he had finished, but he retired to bed with a sense of high accomplish-

ment, and next morning deposited his manuscript with the Eastern Exchange Telegraph
Company before setting out with Mr. Youkoumian for the hills.

The journey was in all respects totally
unlike his narrative. They started, after a
comfortable breakfast, surrounded by the well
wishes of most of the British and many of the
French colony, and instead of riding on camels
they drove in Mr. Kentish's baby Austin. Nor
did they even reach Joab's lair. They had not
gone more than ten miles before a girl appeared
walking alone on the track towards them. She
was not very tidy, particularly about the hair,
but, apart from this, showed every sign of
robust well-being.

" Miss Brooks, I presume," said the journalist, unconsciously following a famous prece-
dent. " But where are the bandits ? "

Prunella looked inquiringly towards Mr.
Youkoumian who, a few steps in the rear, was
shaking his head with vigour. " This British
newspaper writing gentleman," he explained,
" e know all same Matodi gentlemen. E got
the thousand pounds for Joab."

" Well, he'd better take care," said Miss
Brooks, " the bandits are all round you. Oh
you wouldn't see them, of course, but I don't
mind betting that there are fifty rifles covering

us at this moment from behind the boulders and bush and so on." She waved a bare, sun-tanned arm expansively towards the innocent-looking landscape. " I hope you've brought the money in gold."

" It's all here, in the back of the car, Miss Brooks."

" Splendid. Well, I'm afraid Joab won't allow you into his lair, so you and I will wait here, and Youkoumian shall drive into the hills and deliver it."

" But listen, Miss Brooks, my paper has put a lot of money into this story. I got to see that lair."

" I'll tell you all about it," said Prunella, and she did.

" There were three huts," she began, her eyes downcast, her hands folded, her voice precise and gentle as though she were repeating a lesson, " the smallest and the darkest was used as my dungeon."

The journalist shifted uncomfortably. " Huts," he said. " I had formed the impression that they were caves."

" So they were," said Prunella. " Hut is a local word for cave. Two lions were chained beside me night and day. Their eyes glared and I felt their fœtid breath. The chains were of a length so that if I lay perfectly still I was

113

out of their reach. If I had moved hand or foot . . ." She broke off with a little shudder . . .

By the time that Youkoumian returned, the journalist had material for another magnificent front page splash.

" Joab has given orders to withdraw the snipers," Prunella announced, after a whispered consultation with the Armenian. " It is safe for us to go."

So they climbed into the little car and drove unadventurously back to Matodi.

7

Little remains of the story to be told. There was keen enthusiasm in the town when Prunella returned, and an official welcome was organised for her on the subsequent Tuesday. The journalist took many photographs, wrote up a scene of homecoming that stirred the British public to the depths of its heart, and soon flew away in his aeroplane to receive congratulation and promotion at the *Excess* office.

It was expected that Prunella would now make her final choice between Kentish and Benson, but this excitement was denied to the colony. Instead, came the distressing intelli-

gence that she was returning to England. A
light seemed to have been extinguished in
Azanian life, and in spite of avowed good
wishes there was a certain restraint on the eve
of her departure—almost of resentment, as
though Prunella were guilty of disloyalty in
leaving. The *Excess* inserted a paragraph
announcing her arrival, headed ECHO OF
KIDNAPPING CASE, but otherwise she
seemed to have slipped unobtrusively from
public attention. Stebbing, poor fellow, was
obliged to retire from the service. His mind
seemed permanently disordered and from now
on he passed his time, harmlessly but unprofit-
ably, in a private nursing home, working out
hidden messages in Bradshaw's Railway Guide.
Even in Matodi the kidnapping was seldom
discussed.

One day six months later Lepperidge and
Bretherton were sitting in the Club drinking
their evening glass of pink gin. Banditry was
in the air at the moment for that morning the
now memberless trunk of the American missionary had been found at the gates of the Baptist
compound.

" It's one of the problems we shall have to
tackle," said Lepperidge. " A case for action.
I am going to make a report of the entire
matter."

Mr. Brooks passed them on his way out to his lonely dinner table; he was a rare visitor to the club now; the petrol agency was uniformly prosperous and kept him late at his desk. He neither remembered nor regretted his brief popularity, but Lepperidge maintained a guilty cordiality towards him whenever they met.

"Evening, Brooks. Any news of Miss Prunella?"

"Yes, as a matter of fact I heard from her to-day. She's just been married."

"Well I'm blessed . . . I hope you're glad. Anyone we know?"

"Yes, I am glad in a way, though of course I shall miss her. It's that fellow from Kenya who stayed here once; remember him?"

"Ah, yes, him? Well, well . . . Give her my salaams when you write."

Mr. Brooks went downstairs into the still and odorous evening. Lepperidge and Bretherton were completely alone. The Major leant forward and spoke in husky, confidential tones.

"I say, Bretherton," he said, "Look here, there's something I've often wondered, strictly between ourselves, I mean. Did you ever think there was anything fishy about that kidnapping?"

" *Fishy*, sir ? "

" Fishy."

" I think I know what you mean, sir. Well some of us *have* been thinking, lately . . ."

" Exactly."

" Not of course anything definite. Just what you said yourself, sir, *fishy*."

" Exactly . . . Look here, Bretherton, I think you might pass the word round that it's not a thing to be spoken about, see what I mean ? The missus is putting it round to the women too . . ."

" Quite, sir. It's not a thing one wants talked about . . . Arabs, I mean, and frogs."

" Exactly."

There was another long pause. At last Lepperidge rose to go. " I blame myself," he said. "We made a great mistake over that girl. I ought to have known better. After all, first and last when all's said and done, Brooks *is* a commercial wallah."

OUT OF DEPTH

OUT OF DEPTH

I

RIP had got to the decent age when he disliked meeting new people. He lived a contented life between New York and the more American parts of Europe and everywhere, by choosing his season, he found enough of his old acquaintances to keep him effortlessly amused. For fifteen years at least he had dined with Margot Metroland during the first week of his visit to London, and he had always been sure of finding six or eight familiar and welcoming faces. It is true that there were also strangers, but these had passed before him and disappeared from his memory, leaving no more impression than a change of servants at his hotel.

To-night, however, as he entered the drawing-room, before he had greeted his hostess or nodded to Alastair Trumptington, he was aware of something foreign and disturbing. A glance round the assembled party confirmed his alarm. All the men were standing save one; these were mostly old friends interspersed with a handful of new, gawky, wholly inconsiderable young men but the seated figure instantly arrested his attention and froze his bland smile. This was an elderly, large man, quite bald, with a vast white face that spread down and out far beyond the normal limits. It was like Mother Hippo in *Tiger Tim* ; it was like an evening shirt-front in a du Maurier drawing ; down in the depths of the face was a little crimson smirking mouth ; and, above it, eyes that had a shifty, deprecating look, like those of a temporary butler caught out stealing shirts.

Lady Metroland seldom affronted her guests' reticence by introducing them.

" Dear Rip," she said, " it's lovely to see you again. I've got all the gang together for you, you see," and then noticing that his eyes were fixed upon the stranger, added, " Doctor Kakophilos, this is Mr. Van Winkle. Doctor Kakophilos," she added, " is a great magician. Norah brought him, I can't think why."

" Musician ? "

" Magician. Norah says there's nothing he can't do."

" How do you do ? " said Rip.

" Do what thou wilt shall be the whole of law," said Dr. Kakophilos, in a thin Cockney voice.

" Eh ? "

" There is no need to reply. If you wish
to, it is correct to say ' Love is the law, Love
under will.' "

" I see."

" You are unusually blessed. Most men are
blind."

" I tell you what," said Lady Metroland.
" Let's all have some dinner."

It took an hour's substantial eating and
drinking before Rip began to feel at ease
again. He was well placed between two
married women of his own generation, with
both of whom, at one time and another, he
had had affairs ; but even their genial gossip
could not entirely hold his attention and he
found himself continually gazing down the
table to where, ten places away, Dr. Kakophilos
was frightening a pop-eyed débutante out of
all semblance of intelligence. Later, however,
wine and reminiscence began to glow within
him. He remembered that he had been
brought up a Catholic and had therefore no
need to fear black magic. He reflected that
he was wealthy and in good health ; that none
of his women had ever borne him ill-will
(and what better sign of good character was

there than that ?) ; that it was his first week
in London and that everyone he most liked
seemed to be there too ; that the wine was so
copious he had ceased to notice its excellence.
He got going well and soon had six neighbours
listening as he told some successful stories in
his soft, lazy voice ; he became aware with
familiar, electric tremors that he had captured
the attention of a lady opposite on whom he
had had his eye last summer in Venice and
two years before in Paris ; he drank a good
deal more and didn't care a damn for
Dr. Kakophilos.

Presently, almost imperceptibly to Rip, the
ladies left the dining-room. He found himself
with a *ballon* of brandy and a cigar, leaning back
in his chair and talking for about the first time
in his life to Lord Metroland. He was telling
him about big game when he was aware of a
presence at his other side, like a cold draught.
He turned and saw that Dr. Kakophilos had
come sidling up to him.

" You will see me home to-night," said the
magician. " You and Sir Alastair ? "

" Like hell I will," said Rip.

" Like hell," repeated Dr. Kakophilos, deep
meaning resounding through his horrible
Cockney tones. " I have need of you."

" Perhaps we ought to be going up," said

Lord Metroland, " or Margot will get restless."

For Rip the rest of the evening passed in a
pleasant daze. He remembered Margot con-
fiding in him that Norah and that silly little
something girl had had a scene about Dr.
Kakophilos and had both gone home in rages.
Presently the party began to thin until he
found himself alone with Alastair Trumptington
drinking whiskeys in the small drawing-room.
They said good-bye and descended the stairs
arm-in-arm. " I'll drop you, old boy."

" No, old boy, *I'll* drop *you*."

" I like driving at night."

" So do I, old boy."

They were on the steps when a cold Cockney
voice broke in on their friendly discussion.

" Will you please drop *me* ? " A horrible
figure in a black cloak had popped out on
them.

" Where do you want to go ? " asked
Alastair in some distaste.

Dr. Kakophilos gave an obscure address in
Bloomsbury.

" Sorry, old boy, bang out of my way."

" And mine."

" But you said you liked driving at night."

" Oh God ! All right, jump in."

And the three went off together.

Rip never quite knew how it came about that he and Alastair went up to Dr. Kakophilos's sitting-room. It was certainly not for a drink, because there was none there ; nor did he know how it was that Dr. Kakophilos came to be wearing a crimson robe embroidered with gold symbols and a conical crimson hat. It only came to him quite suddenly that Dr. Kakophilos *was* wearing these clothes ; and when it came it set him giggling, so uncontrollably that he had to sit on the bed. And Alastair began to laugh too, and they both sat on the bed for a long time laughing.

But quite suddenly Rip found that they had stopped laughing and that Dr. Kakophilos, still looking supremely ridiculous in his sacerdotal regalia, was talking to them ponderously about time and matter and spirit and a number of things which Rip had got through forty-three eventful years without considering.

" And so," Dr. Kakophilos was saying, " you must breathe the fire and call upon Omraz the spirit of release and journey back through the centuries and recover the garnered wisdom which the ages of reason have wasted. I chose you because you are the two most ignorant men I ever met. I have too much knowledge to risk my safety. If you never come back nothing will be lost."

" Oh, I say," said Alastair.

" And what's more, you're tipsy," said Dr. Kakophilos relapsing suddenly into everyday speech. Then he became poetic again and Rip yawned and Alastair yawned.

At last Rip : " Jolly decent of you to tell us all this, old boy ; I'll come in another time to hear the rest. Must be going now, you know."

" Yes," said Alastair. " A most interesting evening."

Dr. Kakophilos removed his crimson hat and mopped his moist, hairless head. He surveyed his parting guests with undisguised disdain.

" Sots," he said, " You are partakers in a mystery beyond your comprehension. In a few minutes your drunken steps will have straddled the centuries. Tell me, Sir Alastair," he asked, his face alight with ghastly, facetious, courtesy, " Have you any preference with regard to your translation ? You may choose any age you like."

" Oh, I say, jolly decent of you . . . Never was much of a dab at History you know."

" Say."

" Well, any time really. How about

Ethelred the Unready?—always had a soft spot for him."

" And you, Mr. Van Winkle ? "

" Well, if I've got to be moved about, being an American, I'd sooner go forwards—say five hundred years."

Dr. Kakophilos drew himself up. " Do what thou wilt shall be the whole of the law."

" I can answer that one. ' Love is the law, Love under will.' "

" God, we've been a long time in that house," said Alastair as at length they regained the Bentley. " Awful old humbug. Comes of getting tight."

" Hell, I could do with another," said Rip. " Know anywhere ? "

" I do," said Alastair and, turning a corner sharply, ran, broadside on, into a mail van that was thundering down Shaftesbury Avenue at forty-five miles an hour.

When Rip stood up, dazed but, as far as he could judge, without specific injury, he was scarcely at all surprised to observe that both cars had disappeared.

There was so much else to surprise him ; a light breeze, a clear, star-filled sky, a wide horizon unobscured by buildings. The moon,

in her last quarter, hung low above a grove of
trees, illumined a slope of hummocky turf and a
herd of sheep peacefully cropping the sedge
near Piccadilly Circus, and beyond was reflected
in a still pool, pierced here and there with reed.

Instinctively, for his head and eyes were
still aflame from the wine he had drunk and
there was a dry, stale taste in his mouth, Rip
approached the water. His evening shoes
sank deeper with each step and he paused,
uncertain. The entrance of the Underground
Station was there, transformed into a Piranesi
ruin ; a black aperture tufted about with fern
and some crumbling steps leading down to
black water. Eros had gone, but the pedestal
rose above the reeds, moss grown and dilapi-
dated.

" Golly," said Mr. Van Winkle slowly.
" The twenty-fifth century."

Then he crossed the threshold of the underground station and, kneeling on the slippery
fifth step, immersed his head in the water.

Absolute stillness lay all around him except
for rhythmic, barely audible nibbling of the
pastured sheep. Clouds drifted across the
moon and Rip stood awed by the darkness ;
they passed and Rip stepped out into the light,
left the grotto and climbed to a grass mound
at the corner of the Haymarket.

To the south, between the trees, he could pick out the silver line of the river. Warily, for the ground was full of pits and crevices, he crossed what had once been Leicester and Trafalgar Squares. Great flats of mud, submerged at high water, stretched to his feet over the Strand, and at the margin of mud and sedge was a cluster of huts, built on poles; inaccessible because their careful householders had drawn up the ladders at sunset. Two camp fires, almost extinct, glowed red upon platforms of beaten earth. A ragged guard slept with his head on his knees. Two or three dogs prowled below the huts, nosing for refuse, but the breeze was blowing from the river bank and, though Rip had made some noise in his approach, they gave no alarm. Limitless calm lay on all sides among the monstrous shapes of grass-grown masonry and concrete. Rip crouched in a damp hollow and waited for day.

It was still night, darker from the setting of the moon, when the cocks began to crow— twenty or thirty of them, Rip judged—from the roosts under the village. The sentry came to life and raked over the embers sending up a spatter of wood sparks.

Presently a thin line of light appeared downstream, broadening into delicate summer dawn. Birds sang all round him. Tousled households appeared on the little platforms before the huts; women scratching their heads, shaking out blankets, naked children. They let down ladders of hide and stick; two or three women padded down to the river with earthenware pots to draw water; they hitched up their clothes to the waist and waded thigh deep.

From where Rip lay he could see the full extent of the village. The huts extended for half a mile or so, in a single line along the bank. There were about fifty of them; all of the same size and character, built of wattle and mud with skin-lined roofs; they seemed sturdy and in good repair. A dozen or more canoes were beached along the mud flats; some of them dug-out trees, others of a kind of basketwork covered in skins. The people were fair skinned and fair haired, but shaggy, and they moved with the loping gait of savages. They spoke slowly in the sing-song tones of an unlettered race who depend on oral tradition for the preservation of their lore.

Their words seemed familiar yet unintelligible. For more than an hour Rip watched the village come to life and begin the routine of its day, saw the cooking-pots slung over the fires, the men going down and muttering sagely over their boats as longshoremen do; saw the children scrambling down the supports of the houses to the refuse below—and for perhaps the first time in his life felt uncertain of what he should do. Then with as much resolution as he could muster, he walked towards the village.

The effect was instantaneous. There was a general scramble of women for their children, a general stampede for the ladders. The men at the boats stopped fiddling with tackle and came lumbering up the banks. Rip smiled and walked on. The men got together and showed no inclination to budge. Rip raised his clasped hands and shook them amicably in the air as he had seen boxers do when entering the ring. The shaggy white men made no sign of recognition.

"Good morning," said Rip. "Is this London?"

The men looked at each other in surprise, and one very old white beard giggled slightly. After a painful delay the leader nodded and said, ' Lunnon.' Then they cautiously encircled him until, growing bolder, they came right up to him and began to finger his outlandish garments, tapping his crumpled shirt with their horny nails and plucking at his studs and buttons. The women meanwhile were shrieking with excitement in the house-tops. When

Rip looked up to them and smiled, they dodged into the doorways, peeping out at him from the smoky interiors. He felt remarkably foolish and very dizzy. The men were discussing him ; they squatted on their hams and began to debate, without animation or conviction. Occasional phrases came to him, " white," " black boss," " trade," but for the most part the jargon was without meaning. Rip sat down too. The voices rose and fell liturgically. Rip closed his eyes and made a desperate effort to wake himself from this preposterous nightmare. " I am in London, in nineteen-thirty-three, staying at the Ritz Hotel. I drank too much last night at Margot's. Have to go carefully in future. Nothing really wrong. I am in the Ritz in nineteen-thirty-three." He said it over and over again, shutting his senses to all outward impression, forcing his will towards sanity. At last, fully convinced, he raised his head and opened his eyes . . . early morning on the river, a cluster of wattle huts, a circle of impassive barbarous faces . . .

2

It is not to be supposed that one who has lightly skipped five hundred years would take

great notice of the passage of days and nights.
Often in Rip's desultory reading, he had struck
such phrases as, 'From then time ceased to have
any reality for her '; at last he knew what they
meant. There was a time when he lived under
guard among the Londoners ; they fed him on
fish and coarse bread and heady, viscous beer ;
often, in the late afternoon when the work
for the day was over, the village women would
collect round him in a little circle, watching all
his movements with an intent scrutiny ; sometimes impatiently (once a squat young matron
came up to him and suddenly tweaked his hair)
but more often shyly—ready to giggle or take
flight at any unusual movement.

This captivity may have lasted many days.
He was conscious of restraint and strangeness ;
nothing else.

Then there was another impression ; the
coming of the boss. A day of excitement in
the village ; the arrival of a large mechanically
propelled boat, with an awning and a flag ; a
crew of smart negroes, all wearing uniforms of
leather and fur although it was high summer ;
a commander among the negroes issuing orders
in a quiet supercilious voice. The Londoners
brought out sacks from their huts and spread on
the beach the things they had recovered from
the ruins by digging—pieces of machinery and

ornament, china and glass and carved stonework, jewellery and purposeless bits of things they hoped might have value. The blacks landed bales of thick cloth, cooking utensils, fish-hooks, knife-blades and axe-heads; discussion and barter followed, after which the finds from the diggings were bundled up into the launch. Rip was led forward and presented, turned round and inspected; then he too was put in the launch.

A phantasmagoric journey downstream; Rip seated on the cargo; the commander puffing imperturbably at a cigar. Now and then they stopped at other villages, smaller than London, but built on the same plan. Here curious Englishmen crowded the banks and paddled in to stare at him until peremptorily told to keep their distance. The nightmare journey continued.

Arrival at the coast; a large military station; uniforms of leather and fur; black faces; flags; saluting. A pier with a large steamer alongside; barracks and a government house. A negro anthropologist with vast spectacles. Impressions became more vivid and more brief; momentary illumination like flickering lightning. Someone earnestly trying to talk to Rip. Saying English words very slowly; reading to him from a book, familiar words with an extraordinary accent; a black man trying to read Shakespeare to Rip. Someone measured his skull with calipers. Growing blackness and despair; restraint and strangeness; moments of illumination rarer and more fantastic.

At night when Rip woke up and lay alone with his thoughts quite clear and desperate, he said: "This is not a dream. It is simply that I have gone mad." Then more blackness and wildness.

The officers and officials came and went. There was a talk of sending him "home". "Home," thought Rip and beyond the next official town, vague and more distant, he saw the orderly succession of characterless, steam-heated apartments, the cabin trunks and promenade decks, the casinos and bars and supper restaurants, that were his home.

And then later—how much later he could not tell—something that was new and yet ageless. The word "Mission" painted on a board; a black man dressed as a Dominican friar . . . and a growing clearness. Rip knew that out of strangeness, there had come into being something familiar; a shape in chaos. Something was being done. Something was being done that Rip knew; something that twenty-five centuries had not altered; of his own childhood which survived the age of the world. In a log-built church at the coast town he was squatting among a native congregation ; some of them in cast-off uniforms ; the women had shapeless, convent-sewn frocks ; all round him dishevelled white men were staring ahead with vague, uncomprehending eyes, to the end of the room where two candles burned. The priest turned towards them his bland, black face.

" Ite, missa est ".

3

It was some days after the accident before Rip was well enough to talk. Then he asked for the priest who had been by his head when he recovered consciousness.

" What I can't understand, Father, is how you came to be there."

" I was called in to see Sir Alastair. He wasn't badly hurt, but he had been knocked unconscious. You both had a lucky escape. It was odd Sir Alastair asking for me. He isn't a Catholic, but he seems to have had some sort of dream while he was unconscious that made him want to see a priest. Then they told me you were here too, so I came along."

Rip thought for a little. He felt very dizzy when he tried to think.

" Alastair had a dream too, did he ? "

" Apparently something about the Middle Ages.   It made him ask for me."

" Father," said Rip, " I want to make a confession . . . I have experimented in black art . . ."

EXCURSION IN REALITY

I

THE commissionaire at Espinoza's restaurant seems to maintain under his
particular authority all the most decrepit
taxicabs in London. He is a commanding man ;
across his great chest the student of military
medals may construe a tale of heroism and
experience ; Boer farms sink to ashes, fanatical
Fuzzi-wuzzies hurl themselves to paradise,
supercilious mandarins survey the smashing of
their porcelain and rending of fine silk, in that
triple row of decorations. He has only to run
from the steps of Espinoza's to call to your
service a vehicle as crazy as all the enemies of
the King-Emperor.

Half-a-crown into the white cotton glove,
because Simon Lent was too tired to ask for
change. He and Sylvia huddled into the darkness on broken springs, between draughty
windows. It had been an unsatisfactory
evening. They had sat over their table until
two because it was an extension night. Sylvia
would not drink anything because Simon had

141

said he was broke. So they sat for five or six hours, sometimes silent, sometimes bickering, sometimes exchanging listless greetings with the passing couples. Simon dropped Sylvia at her door; a kiss, clumsily offered, coldly accepted; then back to the attic flat, over a sleepless garage, for which Simon paid six guineas a week.

Outside his door they were sluicing a limousine. He squeezed round it and climbed the narrow stairs, that had once echoed to the whistling of ostlers, stamping down to stables before dawn. (Woe to young men in Mewses! Oh woe, to bachelors half in love, living on £800 a year!) There was a small heap of letters on his dressing-table, which had arrived that evening while he was dressing. He lit his gas fire and began to open them. Tailor's bill £56, hosier £43; a reminder that his club subscription for that year had not yet been paid; his account from Espinoza's with a note informing him that the terms were strict, net cash monthly, and that no further credit would be extended to him; it " appeared from the books " of his bank that his last cheque overdrew his account £10 16s. beyond the limit of his guaranteed overdraft; a demand from the income-tax collector for particulars of his employees and their wages (Mrs. Shaw, who came in to make

142

his bed and orange juice for 4s. 6d. a day);
small bills for books, spectacles, cigars, hair
lotion and Sylvia's last four birthday presents.
(Woe to shops that serve young men in
Mewses !)

The other part of his mail was in marked
contrast to this. There was a box of preserved
figs from an admirer in Fresno, California ;
two letters from young ladies who said they
were composing papers about his work for
their college literary societies, and would he
send a photograph ; press cuttings describing
him as a " popular," " brilliant," " meteoric-
ally successful," and " enviable " young
novelist ; a request for the loan of two hundred
pounds from a paralysed journalist ; an invitation to luncheon from Lady Metroland ; six
pages of closely reasoned abuse from a lunatic
asylum in the North of England. For the
truth, which no one who saw into Simon Lent's
heart could possibly have suspected, was that
he was in his way and within his limits quite a
famous young man.

There was a last letter with a typewritten
address which Simon opened with little expectation of pleasure. The paper was headed with
the name of a Film Studio in one of the suburbs
of London. The letter was brief and business-
like.

Dear Simon Lent (a form of address, he had noted before, largely favoured by the theatrical profession),

I wonder whether you have ever considered writing for the Films. We should value your angle on a picture we are now making. Perhaps you would meet me for luncheon to-morrow at the Garrick Club and let me know your reactions to this. Will you leave a message with my night-secretary some time before 8 a.m. to-morrow morning or with my day-secretary after that hour.

Cordially yours,

Below this were two words written in pen and ink which seemed to be *Jewee Mecceee* with below them the explanatory typescript (*Sir James Macrae*).

Simon read this through twice. Then he rang up Sir James Macrae and informed his night-secretary that he would keep the luncheon appointment next day. He had barely put down the telephone before the bell rang.

" This is Sir James Macrae's night-secretary speaking. Sir James would be very pleased if Mr. Lent would come round and see him this evening at his house in Hampstead."

Simon looked at his watch. It was nearly three. " Well . . . it's rather late to go so far to-night . . ."

" Sir James is sending a car for you."

Simon was no longer tired. As he waited for the car the telephone rang again. "Simon," said Sylvia's voice; "are you asleep?"

"No, in fact I'm just going out."

"*Simon* . . . I say, was I beastly to-night?"

"Lousy."

"Well, I thought you were lousy too."

"Never mind. See you sometime."

"Aren't you going to go on talking?"

"Can't, I'm afraid. I've got to do some work."

"*Simon*, what *can* you mean?"

"Can't explain now. There's a car waiting."

"When am I seeing you—to-morrow?"

"Well, I don't really know. Ring me up in the morning. Good night."

A quarter of a mile away, Sylvia put down the telephone, rose from the hearthrug, where she had settled herself in the expectation of twenty minutes' intimate explanation and crept disconsolately into bed.

Simon bowled off to Hampstead through deserted streets. He sat back in the car in a state of pleasant excitement. Presently they began to climb the steep little hill and emerged into an open space with a pond and the tops of trees, black and deep as a jungle in the darkness. The night-butler admitted him to the low Georgian house and led him to the library, where Sir James Macrae was standing before the fire, dressed in ginger-coloured plus fours. A table was laid with supper.

" Evening, Lent. Nice of you to come. Have to fit in business when I can. Cocoa or whisky ? Have some rabbit pie, it's rather good. First chance of a meal I've had since breakfast. Ring for some more cocoa, there's a good chap. Now what was it you wanted to see me about ? "

" Well, I thought *you* wanted to see *me*."

" Did I ? Very likely. Miss Bentham'll know. She arranged the appointment. You might ring the bell on the desk, will you ? "

Simon rang and there instantly appeared the neat night-secretary.

" Miss Bentham, what did I want to see Mr. Lent about ? "

" I'm afraid I couldn't say, Sir James. Miss Harper is responsible for Mr. Lent. When I came on duty this evening I merely found a note from her asking me to fix an appointment as soon as possible."

" Pity," said Sir James. " We'll have to wait until Miss Harper comes on to-morrow."

" I think it was something about writing for films."

" Very likely," said Sir James. " Sure to be

146

something of the kind. I'll let you know without delay. Thanks for dropping in." He put down his cup of cocoa and held out his hand with unaffected cordiality. "Good night, my dear boy." He rang the bell for the night-butler. "Sanders, I want Benson to run Mr. Lent back."

"I'm sorry, sir. Benson has just gone down to the studio to fetch Miss Grits."

"Pity," said Sir James. "Still, I expect you'll be able to pick up a taxi or something."

2

Simon got to bed at half-past four. At ten minutes past eight the telephone by his bed was ringing.

"Mr. Lent? This is Sir James Macrae's secretary speaking. Sir James's car will call for you at half-past eight to take you to the studio."

"I shan't be ready as soon as that, I'm afraid."

There was a shocked pause; then, the day-secretary said: "Very well, Mr. Lent. I will see if some alternative arrangement is possible and ring you in a few minutes."

In the intervening time Simon fell asleep

again. Then the bell woke him once more and the same impersonal voice addressed him.

" Mr. Lent ? I have spoken to Sir James. His car will call for you at eight forty-five."

Simon dressed hastily. Mrs. Shaw had not yet arrived, so there was no breakfast for him. He found some stale cake in the kitchen cupboard and was eating it when Sir James's car arrived. He took a slice down with him, still munching.

" You needn't have brought that " ; said a severe voice from inside the car. " Sir James has sent you some breakfast. Get in quickly ; we're late."

In the corner, huddled in rugs, sat a young woman in a jaunty red hat ; she had bright eyes and a very firm mouth.

" I expect that you are Miss Harper."

" No. I'm Elfreda Grits. We're working together on this film, I believe. I've been up all night with Sir James. If you don't mind I'll go to sleep for twenty minutes. You'll find a thermos of cocoa and some rabbit pie in the basket on the floor."

" Does Sir James live on cocoa and rabbit pie ? "

" No ; those are the remains of his supper. Please don't talk. I want to sleep."

Simon disregarded the pie, but poured some

steaming cocoa into the metal cap of the thermos
flask.   In the corner, Miss Grits composed
herself for sleep. She took off the jaunty red
hat and laid it between them on the seat, veiled
her eyes with two blue-pigmented lids and
allowed the firm lips to relax and gape a little.
Her platinum-blonde wind-swept head bobbed
and swayed with the motion of the car as they
swept out of London through converging and
diverging tram lines.   Stucco gave place to
brick and the façades of the tube stations
changed from tile to concrete ; unoccupied
building plots appeared and newly planted trees
along unnamed avenues. Five minutes exactly
before their arrival at the studio, Miss Grits
opened her eyes, powdered her nose, touched
her lips with red, and pulling her hat on to the
side of her scalp, sat bolt upright, ready for
another day.

Sir James was at work on the lot when they
arrived.   In a white-hot incandescent hell two
young people were carrying on an infinitely
tedious conversation at what was presumably
the table of a restaurant. A dozen emaciated
couples in evening dress danced listlessly
behind them. At the other end of the huge
shed some carpenters were at work building

the façade of a Tudor manor house. Men in
eye-shades scuttled in and out. Notices stood
everywhere. *Do not Smoke. Do not Speak.*
Keep away from the high-power cable.

Miss Grits, in defiance of these regulations,
lit a cigarette, kicked some electric apparatus
out of her path, said, " He's busy. I expect
he'll see us when he's through with this scene,"
and disappeared through a door marked *No*
admittance.

Shortly after eleven o'clock Sir James caught
sight of Simon. " Nice of you to come. Shan't
be long now," he called out to him. " Mr.
Briggs, get a chair for Mr. Lent."

At two o'clock he noticed him again. " Had
any lunch ? "

" No," said Simon.

" No more have I. Just coming."

At half-past three Miss Grits joined him and
said : " Well, it's been an easy day so far.
You mustn't think we're always as slack as this.
There's a canteen across the yard. Come and
have something to eat."

An enormous buffet was full of people in a
variety of costume and make-up. Disappointed
actresses in languorous attitudes served cups of
tea and hard-boiled eggs. Simon and Miss
Grits ordered sandwiches and were about to
eat them when a loud-speaker above their heads

suddenly announced with alarming distinct-
ness, " Sir James Macrae calling Mr. Lent and
Miss Grits in the Conference Room."

" Come on, quick," said Miss Grits. She
bustled him through the swing doors, across
the yard, into the office buildings and up a
flight of stairs to a solid oak door marked
Conference. Keep out.

Too late.

" Sir James has been called away," said the
secretary. " Will you meet him at the West
End office at five-thirty."

Back to London, this time by tube. At
five-thirty they were at the Piccadilly office
ready for the next clue in their treasure hunt.
This took them to Hampstead. Finally at
eight they were back at the studio. Miss
Grits showed no sign of exhaustion.

" Decent of the old boy to give us a day off,"
she remarked. " He's easy to work with in
that way—after Hollywood. Let's get some
supper."

But as they opened the canteen doors and
felt the warm breath of light refreshments,
the loud-speaker again announced : " Sir James
Macrae calling Mr. Lent and Miss Grits in the
Conference Room."

This time they were not too late. Sir James
was there at the head of an oval table ; round

him were grouped the chiefs of his staff. He
sat in a greatcoat with his head hung forward,
elbows on the table and his hands clasped
behind his neck. The staff sat in respectful
sympathy. Presently he looked up, shook
himself and smiled pleasantly.

" Nice of you to come," he said. " Sorry I
couldn't see you before. Lots of small things
to see to on a job like this. Had dinner ? "

" Not yet."

" Pity. Have to eat, you know. Can't work
at full pressure unless you eat plenty."

Then Simon and Miss Grits sat down and
Sir James explained his plan. " I want, ladies
and gentlemen, to introduce Mr. Lent to you.
I'm sure you all know his name already and I
daresay some of you know his work. Well, I've
called him in to help us and I hope that when
he's heard the plan he'll consent to join us. I
want to produce a film of *Hamlet*. I daresay
you don't think that's a very original idea—
but it's Angle that counts in the film world. I'm
going to do it from an entirely new angle.
That's why I've called in Mr. Lent. I want
him to write dialogue for us."

" But, surely," said Simon, " there's quite a
lot of dialogue there already ? "

" Ah, you don't see my angle. There have
been plenty of productions of Shakespeare in

modern dress. We are going to produce him in modern speech. How can you expect the public to enjoy Shakespeare when they can't make head or tail of the dialogue. D'you know I began reading a copy the other day and blessed if *I* could understand it. At once I said, ' What the public wants is Shakespeare with all his beauty of thought and character translated into the language of every day life.' Now Mr. Lent here was the man whose name naturally suggested itself. Many of the most high-class critics have commended Mr. Lent's dialogue. Now my idea is that Miss Grits here shall act in an advisory capacity, helping with the continuity and the technical side, and that Mr. Lent shall be given a free hand with the scenario . . ."

The discourse lasted for a quarter of an hour; then the chiefs of staff nodded sagely; Simon was taken into another room and given a contract to sign by which he received £50 a week retaining fee and £250 advance.

" You had better fix up with Miss Grits the times of work most suitable to you. I shall expect your first treatment by the end of the week. I should go and get some dinner if I were you. Must eat."

Slightly dizzy, Simon hurried to the canteen

where two languorous blondes were packing up for the night.

"We've been on since four o'clock this morning," they said, "and the supers have eaten everything except the nougat. Sorry."

Sucking a bar of nougat Simon emerged into the now deserted studio. On three sides of him, to the height of twelve feet, rose in appalling completeness the marble walls of the scene-restaurant; at his elbow a bottle of imitation champagne still stood in its pail of melted ice; above and beyond extended the vast gloom of rafters and ceiling.

"*Fact*," said Simon to himself, "the world of action . . . the pulse of life . . . Money, hunger . . . *Reality*."

Next morning he was called with the words, "Two young ladies waiting to see you."

"Two?"

Simon put on his dressing-gown and, orange juice in hand, entered his sitting-room. Miss Grits nodded pleasantly.

"We arranged to start at ten," she said. "But it doesn't really matter. I shall not require you very much in the early stages. This is Miss Dawkins. She is one of the staff stenographers. Sir James thought you would

need one. Miss Dawkins will be attached to
you until further notice. He also sent two
copies of *Hamlet*. When you've had your
bath, I'll read you my notes for our first
treatment."

But this was not to be; before Simon was
dressed Miss Grits had been recalled to the
studio on urgent business.

" I'll ring up and tell you when I am free,"
she said.

Simon spent the morning dictating letters to
everyone he could think of; they began—
*Please forgive me for dictating this, but I am so
busy just now that I have little time for personal
correspondence . . .*" Miss Dawkins sat
deferentially over her pad. He gave her
Sylvia's number.

" Will you get on to this number and present
my compliments to Miss Lennox and ask
her to luncheon at Espinoza's . . . And book
a table for two there at one forty-five."

" Darling," said Sylvia, when they met,
" why were you out all yesterday and *who* was
that voice this morning ? "

" Oh, that was Miss Dawkins, my steno-
grapher."

" Simon, what *can* you mean ? "

" You see, I've joined the film industry."

" *Darling*. Do give me a job."

"Well, I'm not paying much attention to casting at the moment—but I'll bear you in mind."

"Goodness. How you've changed in two days!"

"Yes!" said Simon, with great complacency. "Yes, I think I have. You see, for the first time in my life I have come into contact with Real Life. I'm going to give up writing novels. It was a mug's game anyway. The written word is dead—first the papyrus, then the printed book, now the film. The artist must no longer work alone. He is part of the age in which he lives; he must share (only of course, my dear Sylvia, in very different proportions) the weekly wage envelope of the proletarian. Vital art implies a corresponding set of social relationships. Co-operation . . . co-ordination . . . the hive endeavour of the community directed to a single end . . ."

Simon continued in this strain at some length, eating meantime a luncheon of Dickensian dimensions, until, in a small, miserable voice, Sylvia said : " It seems to me that you've fallen for some ghastly film star."

" O God," said Simon, " only a virgin could be as vulgar as that."

They were about to start one of their old, interminable quarrels when the telephone boy brought a message that Miss Grits wished to resume work instantly.

" So that's her name," said Sylvia.

" If you only knew how funny that was," said Simon, scribbling his initials on the bill and leaving the table while Sylvia was still groping with gloves and bag.

As things turned out, however, he became Miss Grits' lover before the week was out. The idea was hers. She suggested it to him one evening at his flat as they corrected the typescript of the final version of their first treatment.

" No, really," Simon said aghast. " No, really. It would be quite impossible. I'm sorry, but . . ."

" Why ?   Don't you like women ? "

" Yes, but . . ."

" Oh, come along," Miss Grits said briskly. " We don't get much time for amusement . . ." And later, as she packed their manuscripts into her attaché case she said, " We must do it again if we have time.   Besides I find it's so much easier to work with a man if you're having an *affaire* with him."

3

For three weeks Simon and Miss Grits (he always thought of her by this name in spite of all subsequent intimacies) worked together in complete harmony. His life was re-directed and transfigured. No longer did he lie in bed, glumly preparing himself for the coming day; no longer did he say every morning 'I *must* get down to the country and finish that book' and every evening find himself slinking back to the same urban flat; no longer did he sit over supper tables with Sylvia, idly bickering; no more listless explanations over the telephone. Instead he pursued a routine of incalculable variety, summoned by telephone at all hours to conferences which rarely assembled; sometimes to Hampstead, sometimes to the studios, once to Brighton. He spent long periods of work pacing up and down his sitting-room, with Miss Grits pacing backwards and forwards along the other wall and Miss Dawkins obediently perched between them, as the two dictated, corrected and redrafted their scenario. There were meals at improbable times and vivid, unsentimental passages of love with Miss Grits. He ate irregular and improbable meals, bowling through the suburbs in Sir James's car, pacing the carpet dictating to Miss Dawkins, perched in deserted lots upon scenery which seemed made to survive the collapse of.civilisation. He lapsed, like Miss Grits, into brief spells of death-like unconsciousness, often awakening, startled, to find that a street or desert or factory had come into being about him while he slept.

The film meanwhile grew rapidly, daily putting out new shoots and changing under their eyes in a hundred unexpected ways. Each conference produced some radical change in the story. Miss Grits in her precise, unvariable voice would read out the fruits of their work. Sir James would sit with his head in his hand, rocking slightly from side to side and giving vent to occasional low moans and whimpers; round him sat the experts—production, direction, casting, continuity, cutting and costing managers, bright eyes, eager to attract the great man's attention with some apt intrusion.

"Well," Sir James would say, "I think we can O.K. that. Any suggestions, gentlemen?"

There would be a pause, until one by one the experts began to deliver their contributions ... " I've been thinking, sir, that it won't do to have the scene laid in Denmark. The public won't stand for travel stuff. How about setting it in Scotland—then we could have some kilts and clan gathering scenes?"

"Yes, that's a very sensible suggestion. Make a note of that, Lent ..."

" I was thinking we'd better drop this character of the Queen. She'd much better be dead before the action starts. She hangs up the action. The public won't stand for him abusing his mother."

" Yes, make a note of that, Lent."

" How would it be, sir, to make the ghost the Queen instead of the King . . ."

" Yes, make a note of that Lent . . ."

" Don't you think, sir, it would be better if Ophelia were Horatio's sister. More poignant, if you see what I mean."

" Yes, make a note of that . . ."

" I think we are losing sight of the essence of the story in the last sequence. After all, it is first and foremost a Ghost Story, isn't it ? . . ."

And so from simple beginnings the story spread majestically. It was in the second week that Sir James, after, it must be admitted, considerable debate, adopted the idea of incorporating with it the story of *Macbeth*. Simon was opposed to the proposition at first, but the appeal of the three witches proved too strong. The title was then changed to *The White Lady of Dunsinane*, and he and Miss Grits settled down to a prodigious week's work in rewriting their entire scenarios.

4

The end came as suddenly as everything else in this remarkable episode. The third conference was being held at an hotel in the New Forest where Sir James happened to be staying; the experts had assembled by train, car and motor-bicycle at a moment's notice and were tired and unresponsive. Miss Grits read the latest scenario; it took some time, for it had now reached the stage when it could be taken as " white script " ready for shooting. Sir James sat sunk in reflection longer than usual. When he raised his head, it was to utter the single word:

" No."

" No ? "

" No, it won't do. We must scrap the whole thing. We've got much too far from the original story. I can't think why you need introduce Julius Cæsar and King Arthur at all."

" But, sir, they were your own suggestions at the last conference."

" Were they ? Well, I can't help it. I must have been tired and not paying full attention . . . Besides, I don't like the dialogue. It misses all the poetry of the original. What the public wants is Shakespeare, the whole of Shakespeare and nothing but Shakespeare.

Now this scenario you've written is all very well in its way—but it's not Shakespeare. I'll tell you what we'll do. We'll use the play exactly as he wrote it and record from that. Make a note of it, Miss Grits."

" Then you'll hardly require my services any more ? " said Simon.

" No, I don't think I shall. Still, nice of you to have come."

Next morning Simon woke bright and cheerful as usual and was about to leap from his bed when he suddenly remembered the events of last night. There was nothing for him to do. An empty day lay before him. No Miss Grits, no Miss Dawkins, no scampering off to conferences or dictating of dialogue. He rang up Miss Grits and asked her to lunch with him.

" No, quite impossible, I'm afraid. I have to do the continuity for a scenario of St. John's Gospel before the end of the week. Pretty tough job. We're setting it in Algeria so as to get the atmosphere. Off to Hollywood next month. Don't suppose I shall see you again. Good-bye."

Simon lay in bed with all his energy slowly slipping away. Nothing to do. Well, he supposed, now was the time to go away to the country and get on with his novel. Or should he go abroad ? Some quiet café-restaurant in the sun where he could work out those intract-

able last chapters. That was what he would do
. . . sometime . . . the end of the week
perhaps.

Meanwhile he leaned over on his elbow,
lifted the telephone and, asking for Sylvia's
number, prepared himself for twenty-five
minutes' acrimonious reconciliation.

LOVE IN THE SLUMP

I

THE marriage of Tom Watch and Angela Trench-Troubridge was, perhaps, as unimportant an event as has occurred within living memory. No feature was lacking in the previous histories of the two young people, in their engagement, or their wedding, that could make them completely typical of all that was most unremarkable in modern social conditions. The evening paper recorded:

" This has been a busy week at St. Margaret's. The third fashionable wedding of the week took place there this afternoon, between Mr. Tom Watch and Miss Angela Trench-Troubridge. Mr. Watch, who, like so many young men nowadays, works in the city, is the second son of the late Hon. Wilfrid Watch of Holyborne House, Shaftesbury; the bride's father, Colonel Trench-Troubridge is well known as a sportsman, and has stood several times for Parliament in the Conservative interest. Mr. Watch's brother, Captain Peter Watch of the Coldstream Guards, acted as best

167

man. The bride wore a veil of old Brussels lace
lent by her grandmother. In accordance with
the new fashion for taking holidays in Britain,
the bride and bridegroom are spending a
patriotic honeymoon in the West of England."

And when that has been said there is really
very little that need be added.

Angela was twenty-five, pretty, good-natured,
lively, intelligent and popular—just the sort
of girl, in fact, who, for some mysterious cause
deep-rooted in Anglo-Saxon psychology, finds
it most difficult to get satisfactorily married.
During the last seven years she had done
everything which it is customary for girls of
her sort to do. In London she had danced on
an average four evenings a week, for the first
three years at private houses, for the last four
at restaurants and night-clubs ; in the country
she had been slightly patronising to the neighbours and had taken parties to the hunt ball
which she hoped would shock them ; she had
worked in a slum and a hat shop, had published
a novel, been bridesmaid eleven times and godmother once ; been in love, unsuitably, twice ;
had sold her photograph for fifty guineas to
the advertising department of a firm of beauty
specialists ; had got into trouble when her name
was mentioned in gossip columns ; had acted
in five or six charity matinées and two pageants,

had canvassed for the Conservative candidate at two General Elections, and, like every girl in the British Isles, was unhappy at home.

In the Crisis years things became unendurable. For some time her father had shown an increasing reluctance to open the London house; now he began to talk in a sinister way about "economies," by which he meant retiring permanently to the country, reducing the number of indoor servants, stopping bedroom fires, cutting down Angela's allowance and purchasing a mile and a half of fishing in the neighbourhood, on which he had had his eye for several years.

Faced with the grim prospect of.an indefinitely prolonged residence in the home of her ancestors, Angela, like many a sensible English girl before her, decided that after her two unhappy affairs she was unlikely to fall in love again. There was for her no romantic parting of the ways between love and fortune. Elder sons were scarcer than ever that year and there was hot competition from America and the Dominions. The choice was between discomfort with her parents in a Stately Home or discomfort with a husband in a London mews.

Poor Tom Watch had been mildly attentive to Angela since her first season. He was her male counterpart in about every particular.

Normally educated, he had, after taking a Third in History at the University, gone into the office of a reliable firm of chartered accountants, with whom he had worked ever since. And throughout those sunless city afternoons he looked back wistfully to his undergraduate days, when he had happily followed the normal routine of University success by riding second on a borrowed hunter in the Christ Church " grind ", breaking furniture with the Bullingdon, returning at dawn through the window after dances in London, and sharing dingy but expensive lodgings in the High with young men richer than himself.

Angela, as one of the popular girls of her year, used to be a frequent visitor to Oxford and to the houses where Tom stayed during the vacation, and as the bleak succession of years in his accountant's office sobered and depressed him, Tom began to look upon her as one of the few bright fragments remaining from his glamorous past. He still went out a little, for an unattached young man is never quite valueless in London, but the late dinner parties to which he went sulkily, tired by his day's work and out of touch with the topics in which the débutantes attempted to interest him, served only to show him the gulf that was widening between himself and his former friends.

Angela, because (as cannot be made too clear) she was a thoroughly nice girl, was always charming to him, and he returned her interest gratefully. She was, however, a part of his past, not of his future. His regard was sentimental but quite unaspiring. She was a piece of his irrecapturable youth ; nothing could have been more remote from his attitude than to think of her as a possible companion for old age. Accordingly her proposal of marriage came to him as a surprise that was by no means welcome.

They had left a particularly crowded and dull dance, and were eating kippers at a night-club. They were in the intimate and slightly tender mood which always developed between them when Angela had said in a gentle voice :

" You're always so much nicer to me than anyone else, Tom ; I wonder why ? " and before he could deflect her—he had had an unusually exacting day's business and the dance had been stupefying—she had popped the question.

" Well, of course," he had stammered, " I mean to say there's nothing I'd like more, old girl. I mean, you know, of course I've always been crazy about you . . . But the difficulty is I simply can't afford to marry. Absolutely out of the question for years, you know."

"But I don't think I should mind being poor with you, Tom; we know each other so well. Everything would be easy."

And before Tom knew whether he was pleased or not, the engagement had been announced.

He was making eight hundred a year; Angela had two hundred. There was "more coming" to both of them eventually. Things were not too bad if they were sensible about not having children. He would have to give up his occasional days of hunting; she was to give up her maid. On this basis of mutual sacrifice they arranged for their future.

It rained heavily on the day of the wedding, and only the last-ditchers among the St. Margaret's crowd turned out to watch the melancholy succession of guests popping out of their dripping cars and plunging up the covered way into the church. There was a party afterwards at Angela's home in Egerton Gardens. At half-past four, the young couple caught a train at Paddington for the West of England. The blue carpet and the striped awning were rolled away and locked among candle-ends and hassocks in the church store-room. The lights in the aisles were turned out and the doors locked and bolted. The flowers and shrubs were stacked up to await distribu-

tion in the wards of a hospital for incurables
in which Mrs. Watch had an interest. Mrs.
Trench-Troubridge's secretary set to work
dispatching silver-and-white cardboard packets
of wedding cake to servants and tenants in the
country. One of the ushers hurried to Covent
Garden to return his morning coat to the firm
of gentlemen's outfitters from whom it was
hired. A doctor was summoned to attend the
bridegroom's small nephew, who, after attract-
ing considerable attention as page at the ceremony by his outspoken comments, developed
a high temperature and numerous disquieting
symptoms of food-poisoning. Sarah Trum-
pery's maid discreetly returned the travelling
clock which the old lady had inadvertently
pouched from among the wedding presents.
(This foible of hers was well known and the
detectives had standing orders to avoid a
scene at the reception. It was not often that
she was asked to weddings nowadays. When
she was, the stolen presents were invariably
returned that evening or on the following day.)
The bridesmaids got together over dinner and
fell into eager conjecture about the intimacies
of the honeymoon, the odds in this case
being three to two that the ceremony had
not been anticipated. The Great Western
express rattled through the sodden English

LOVE IN THE SLUMP

counties. Tom and Angela sat glumly in
a first-class smoking carriage, discussing the
day.

" It was so wonderful neither of us being
late."

" Mother fussed so . . ."

" I didn't see John, did you ? "

" He was there. He said good-bye to us in
the hall."

" Oh, yes . . . I hope they've packed
everything."

" What books did you bring ? "

A thoroughly normal, uneventful wedding.

Presently Tom said : " I suppose in a way
it's rather unenterprising of us, just going off
to Aunt Martha's house in Devon. Remember
how the Lockwoods went to Morocco and got
captured by brigands ? "

" And the Randalls got snowed up for ten
days in Norway."

" We shan't get much adventure in Devon,
I'm afraid."

" Well, Tom, we haven't really married for
adventure, have we ? "

And, as things happened, it was from that
moment onwards that the honeymoon took an
odd turn.

2

" D'you know if we change ? "

" I rather think we do. I forgot to ask.
Peter got the tickets. I'll get out at Exeter
and find out."

The train drew into the station.

" Shan't be a minute," said Tom, shutting
the door behind him to keep out the cold.
He walked up the platform, purchased a
West country evening paper, learned that
they need not change and was returning to
his carriage when his arm was seized and a
voice said :

" Hello, Watch, old man ! Remember
me ? " And with a little difficulty he recognised
the smiling face of an old school acquaintance.
" See you've just got married. Congratulations.
Meant to write. Great luck running into you
like this. Come and have a drink."

" Wish I could. Got to get back to the
train."

" Heaps of time, old man. Waits twelve
minutes here. Must have a drink."

Still searching his memory for the name of
his old friend, Tom went with him to the
station buffet.

" I live fifteen miles out, you know. Just
come in to meet the train. Expecting some

cow-cake down from London. No sign of it
. . . Well, all the best."

They drank two glasses of whisky—very
comforting after the cold train journey. Then
Tom said :

"Well, it's been jolly seeing you. I must
get back to the train now. Come with me and
meet my wife."

But when they reached the platform, the
train was gone.

"I say, old man, that's darned funny, you
know. What are you going to do ? There's
not another train to-night. Tell you what,
you'd better come and spend the night with me
and go on in the morning. We can wire and
tell your wife where you are."

"I suppose Angela will be all right ? "

"Heavens, yes ! Nothing can happen in
England. Besides, there's nothing you can do.
Give me her address and I'll send a wire now,
telling her where you are. Jump into the car
and wait."

Next morning Tom woke up with a feeling
of slight apprehension. He turned over in bed,
examining with sleepy eyes the unaccustomed
furniture of the room. Then he remembered.
Of course he was married. And Angela had
gone off in the train, and he had driven for
miles in the dark to the house of an old friend

whose name he could not remember. It had
been dinner-time when they arrived. They had
drunk Burgundy and port and brandy. Frankly,
they had drunk rather a lot. They had recalled
numerous house scandals, all kinds of jolly
insults to chemistry masters, escapades after
dark when they had gone up to London to the
" 43." What was the fellow's name ? It was
clearly too late to ask him now. And anyway he
would have to get on to Angela. He supposed
that she had reached Aunt Martha's house
safely and had got his telegram. Awkward
beginning to the honeymoon—but then he and
Angela knew each other so well . . . It was
not as though this were some sudden romance.

Presently he was called. " Hounds are
meeting near here this morning, sir. The
Captain wondered if you'd care to go hunting."

" No, no ! I have to leave immediately after
breakfast."

" The Captain said he could mount you, sir,
and lend you clothes."

" No, no ! Quite impossible."

But when he came down to breakfast and
found his host filling a saddle flask with cherry-
brandy, secret threads began to pull at Tom's
heart.

" Of course we're a comic sort of pack.
Everyone turns out, parson, farmers, all kinds

of animals. But we generally get a decent run along the edge of the moor. Pity you can't come out. I'd like you to try my new mare, she's a lovely ride . . . a bit fine for this type of country, perhaps . . ."

Well, why not ? . . . after all, he and Angela knew each other so well . . . it was not as though . . .

And two hours later Tom found himself in a high wind galloping madly across the worst hunting country in the British Isles—alternations of heather and bog, broken by pot-holes, boulders, mountain streams and dis-used gravel pits—hounds streaming up the valley opposite, the mare going perfectly, farmers' boys on shaggy little ponies, solicitors' wives on cobs, retired old sea-captains bouncing about eighteen hands high, vets and vicars plunging on all sides of him, and not a care in his heart.

Two hours later still he was in less happy circumstances, seated alone in the heather, surrounded on all sides by an unbroken horizon of empty moor. He had dismounted to tighten a girth, and galloping across a hillside to catch up with the field, his mount had put her foot in a rabbit hole, tumbled over, rolled perilously near him, and then regaining her feet, had made off at a brisk canter towards her stable, leaving him on his back, panting for breath. Now he was quite alone in a totally strange country. He did not know the name of his host or of his host's house. He pictured himself tramping from village to village saying : " Can you tell me the address of a young man who was hunting this morning ? He was in Butcher's house at Eton ! " Moreover, Tom suddenly remembered he was married. Of course he and Angela knew each other so well . . . but there were limits.

At eight o'clock that evening a weary figure trudged into the gas-lit parlour of the Royal George Hotel, Chagford. He wore sodden riding boots and torn and muddy clothes. He had wandered for five hours over the moor, and was hungry. They provided him with Canadian cheese, margarine, tinned salmon, and bottled stout, and sent him to sleep in a large brass bedstead which creaked as he moved. But he slept until half-past ten next morning.

The third day of the honeymoon started more propitiously. A bleak sun was shining a little. Stiff and sore in every muscle, Tom dressed in the still damp riding clothes of his unknown host and made inquiries about

reaching the remote village where his Aunt
Martha's house stood, and where Angela
must be anxiously awaiting him. He wired
to her: " *Arriving this evening. Will explain.
All love,*" and then inquired about trains.
There was one train in the day which left early
in the afternoon and, after three changes,
brought him to a neighbouring station late
that evening. Here he suffered another check.
There was no car to be hired in the village.
His aunt's house was eight miles away. The
telephone did not function after seven o'clock.
The day's journey in damp clothes had set
him shivering and sneezing. He was clearly
in for a bad cold. The prospect of eight miles'
walk in the dark was unthinkable. He spent
the night at the inn.

The fourth day dawned to find Tom speech-
less and nearly deaf. In this condition the
car came to conduct him to the house so kindly
lent for his week's honeymoon. Here he was
greeted with the news that Angela had left
early that morning.

" Mrs. Watch received a telegram, sir,
saying that you had met with an accident
hunting. She was very put out as she had
asked several friends to luncheon."

" But where has she gone ? "

" The address was on the telegram, sir. It

was the same address as your first telegram . . .
No, sir, the telegram has not been preserved."

So Angela had gone to his host near Exeter ;
well, she could jolly well look after herself.
Tom felt far too ill to worry. He went straight
to bed.

The fifth day passed in a stupor of misery.
Tom lay in bed listlessly turning the pages of
such books as his aunt had collected in her
fifty years of vigorous out-of-door life. On the
sixth day conscience began to disturb him.
Perhaps he ought to do something about
Angela. It was then the butler suggested that
the name in the inside pocket of the hunting
coat would probably be that of Tom's late,
Angela's present host. Some work with a
local directory settled the matter. He sent a
telegram.

"*Are you all right? Awaiting you here.
Tom,*" and received the answer :

"*Quite all right. Your friend divine. Why
not join us here. Angela.*"

"*In bed severe cold. Tom.*"

"*So sorry darling. Will see you in London or
shall I join you. Hardly worth it is it. Angela.*"

" *Will see you London.   Tom.* "

Of course Angela and he knew each other
very well . . .

Two days later they met in the little flat
which Mrs. Watch had been decorating for
them.
" I hope you've brought all the luggage."
" Yes, darling.   What fun to be home l "
" Office to-morrow."
" Yes, and I've got hundreds of people to
ring up.   I haven't thanked them for the last
batch of presents yet."
" Have a good time ? "
" Not bad.   How's your cold ? "
" Better.   What are we doing to-night ? "
" I promised to go and see mama.   Then I
said I would dine with your Devon friend.   He
came up with me to see about some cow-cake.
It seemed only decent to take him out after
staying with him."
" Quite right.   But I think I won't come."
" No, I shouldn't.   I shall have heaps to tell
her that would bore you."
That evening Mrs. Trench-Troubridge said :
" I thought Angela was looking sweet to-night.

The honeymoon's done her good. So sensible of Tom not to take her on some exhausting trip on the Continent. You can see she's come back quite rested. And the honeymoon is so often such a difficult time particularly after all the rush of the wedding."

"What's this about their taking a cottage in Devon ?" asked her husband.

"Not *taking* dear, it's being given them. Near the house of a bachelor friend of Tom's apparently. Angela said it would be such a good place for her to go sometimes when she wanted a change. They can never get a proper holiday because of Tom's work."

"Very sensible, very sensible indeed," said Mr. Trench-Troubridge, lapsing into a light doze, as was usual with him at nine in the evening.

BELLA FLEACE GAVE A PARTY

BALLINGAR is four and a half hours from Dublin if you catch the early train from Broadstone Station and five and a quarter if you wait until the afternoon. It is the market town of a large and comparatively well-populated district. There is a pretty Protestant Church in 1820 Gothic on one side of the square and a vast, unfinished Catholic cathedral opposite it, conceived in that irresponsible medley of architectural orders that is so dear to the hearts of transmontane pietists. Celtic lettering of a sort is beginning to take the place of the Latin alphabet on the shop fronts that complete the square. These all deal in identical goods in varying degrees of dilapidation ; Mulligan's Store, Flannigan's Store, Riley's Store, each sells thick black boots, hanging in bundles, soapy colonial cheese, hardware and haberdashery, oil and saddlery, and each is licensed to sell ale and porter for consumption on or off the premises. The shell of the barracks stands with empty window frames and blackened interior as a monument to emancipation. Someone has written *The Pope is a Traitor* in tar on the green pillar box. A typical Irish town.

Fleacetown is fifteen miles from Ballingar, on a direct uneven road through typical Irish country; vague purple hills in the far distance and towards them, on one side of the road, fitfully visible among drifting patches of white mist, unbroken miles of bog, dotted with occasional stacks of cut peat. On the other side the ground slopes up to the north, divided irregularly into spare fields by banks and stone walls over which the Ballingar hounds have some of their most eventful hunting. Moss lies on everything; in a rough green rug on the walls and banks, soft green velvet on the timber—blurring the transitions so that there is no knowing where the ground ends and trunk and masonry begin. All the way from Ballingar there is a succession of whitewashed cabins and a dozen or so fair-size farmhouses; but there is no gentleman's house, for all this was Fleace property in the days before the Land Commission. The demesne land is all that belongs to Fleacetown now, and this is let for pasture to neighbouring farmers. Only a few beds are cultivated in the walled kitchen garden; the rest has run to rot, thorned bushes barren of edible fruit spreading everywhere among weedy flowers reverting rankly to type. The hot-houses have been draughty skeletons for ten years. The great gates set in their Georgian arch are permanently padlocked, the lodges are derelict, and the line of the main drive is only just discernible through the meadows. Access to the house is half a mile further up through a farm gate, along a track befouled by cattle.

But the house itself, at the date with which we are dealing, was in a condition of comparatively good repair; compared, that is to say, with Ballingar House or Castle Boycott or Knode Hall. It did not, of course, set up to rival Gordontown, where the American Lady Gordon had installed electric light, central heating and a lift, or Mock House or Newhill, which were leased to sporting Englishmen, or Castle Mockstock, since Lord Mockstock married beneath him. These four houses with their neatly raked gravel, bathrooms and dynamos, were the wonder and ridicule of the country. But Fleacetown, in fair competition with the essentially Irish houses of the Free State, was unusually habitable.

Its roof was intact; and it is the roof which makes the difference between the second and third grade of Irish country houses. Once that goes you have moss in the bedrooms, ferns on the stairs and cows in the library, and in a very few years you have to move into the dairy or one of the lodges. But so long as he has, literally, a roof over his head, an Irishman's house is still his castle. There were weak bits in Fleacetown, but general opinion held that the leads were good for another twenty years and would certainly survive the present owner.

Miss Annabel Rochfort-Doyle-Fleace, to give her the full name under which she appeared in books of reference, though she was known to the entire countryside as Bella Fleace, was the last of her family. There had been Fleaces and Fleysers living about Ballingar since the days of Strongbow, and farm buildings marked the spot where they had inhabited a stockaded fort two centuries before the immigration of the Boycotts or Gordons or Mockstocks. A family tree emblazed by a nineteenth-century genealogist, showing how the original stock had merged with the equally ancient Rochforts and the respectable though more recent Doyles, hung in the billiard-room. The present home had been built on extravagant lines in the middle of the eighteenth century, when the family, though enervated, was still wealthy and influential. It would be tedious to trace its gradual decline from fortune; enough to say that it was due to no heroic debauchery. The Fleaces just got unobtrusively poorer in the way that families do who make no effort to help themselves. In the last generations, too, there had been marked traces of eccentricity. Bella Fleace's mother—an O'Hara of Newhill—had from the day of her marriage until her death suffered from the delusion that she was a negress. Her brother, from whom she had inherited, devoted himself to oil painting; his mind ran on the simple subject of assassination and before his death he had executed pictures of practically every such incident in history from Julius Cæsar to General Wilson. He was at work on a painting, his own murder, at the time of the troubles, when he was, in fact, ambushed and done to death with a shot-gun on his own drive.

It was under one of her brother's paintings—Abraham Lincoln in his box at the theatre—that Miss Fleace was sitting one colourless morning in November when the idea came to her to give a Christmas party. It would be unnecessary to describe her appearance closely, and somewhat confusing, because it seemed in contradiction to much of her character. She was over eighty, very untidy and very red; streaky grey hair was twisted behind her head into a horsy bun, wisps hung round her cheeks; her nose was prominent and blue veined; her eyes pale blue, blank and mad; she had a lively smile and spoke with a marked Irish intonation. She walked with the aid of a stick, having been lamed many years back when her horse rolled her among loose stones late in a long day with the Ballingar Hounds ; a tipsy sporting doctor had completed the mischief, and she had not been able to ride again. She would appear on foot when hounds drew the Fleacetown coverts and loudly criticise the conduct of the huntsman, but every year fewer of her old friends turned out ; strange faces appeared.

They knew Bella, though she did not know them. She had become a by-word in the neighbourhood, a much-valued joke.

" A rotten day," they would report. " We found our fox, but lost again almost at once. But we saw Bella. Wonder how long the old girl will last. She must be nearly ninety. My father remembers when she used to hunt —went like smoke, too."

Indeed, Bella herself was becoming increasingly occupied with the prospect of death. In the winter before the one we are talking of, she had been extremely ill. She emerged in April, rosy cheeked as ever, but slower in her movements and mind. She gave instructions that better attention must be paid to her father's and brother's graves, and in June took the unprecedented step of inviting her heir to visit her. She had always refused to see this young man up till now. He was an Englishman, a very distant cousin, named Banks. He lived in South Kensington and occupied himself in the Museum. He arrived in August and wrote long and very amusing letters to all his friends describing his visit, and later translated his experiences into a short story for the *Spectator*. Bella disliked him from the moment he arrived. He had horn-rimmed spectacles and a B.B.C. voice. He spent most of his time photographing the Fleacetown chimney-pieces and the moulding of the doors. One day he came to Bella bearing a pile of calf-bound volumes from the library.

" I say, did you know you had these ? " he asked.

" I did," Bella lied.

" All first editions. They must be extremely valuable."

" You put them back where you found them."

Later, when he wrote to thank her for his visit—enclosing prints of some of his photographs—he mentioned the books again. This set Bella thinking. Why should that young puppy go poking round the house putting a price on everything ? She wasn't dead yet, Bella thought. And the more she thought of it, the more repugnant it became to think of

Archie Banks carrying off her books to South
Kensington and removing the chimney-pieces
and, as he threatened, writing an essay about
the house for the *Architectural Review*. She
had often heard that the books were valuable.
Well, there were plenty of books in the library
and she did not see why Archie Banks should
profit by them. So she wrote a letter to a
Dublin bookseller. He came to look through
the library, and after a while he offered her
twelve hundred pounds for the lot, or a thousand for the six books which had attracted
Archie Banks' attention. Bella was not sure
that she had the right to sell things out of the
house ; a wholesale clearance would be noticed.
So she kept the sermons and military history
which made up most of the collection, the
Dublin bookseller went off with the first
editions, which eventually fetched rather less
than he had given, and Bella was left with
winter coming on and a thousand pounds in
hand.

It was then that it occurred to her to give
a party. There were always several parties
given round Ballingar at Christmas time, but
of late years Bella had not been invited to any,
partly because many of her neighbours had
never spoken to her, partly because they
did not think she would want to come, and

partly because they would not have known what to do with her if she had. As a matter of fact she loved parties. She liked sitting down to supper in a noisy room, she liked dance music and gossip about which of the girls was pretty and who was in love with them, and she liked drink and having things brought to her by men in pink evening coats. And though she tried to console herself with contemptuous reflections about the ancestry of the hostesses, it annoyed her very much whenever she heard of a party being given in the neighbourhood to which she was not asked.

And so it came about that, sitting with the *Irish Times* under the picture of Abraham Lincoln and gazing across the bare trees of the park to the hills beyond, Bella took it into her head to give a party. She rose immediately and hobbled across the room to the bell-rope. Presently her butler came into the morning room ; he wore the green baize apron in which he cleaned the silver and in his hand he carried the plate brush to emphasise the irregularity of the summons.

" Was it yourself ringing ? " he asked.

" It was, who else ? "

" And I at the silver ! "

" Riley," said Bella with some solemnity, " I propose to give a ball at Christmas."

" Indeed ! " said her butler. " And for what would you want to be dancing at your age ? " But as Bella adumbrated her idea, a sympathetic light began to glitter in Riley's eye.

" There's not been such a ball in the country for twenty-five years. It will cost a fortune."

" It will cost a thousand pounds," said Bella proudly.

The preparations were necessarily stupendous. Seven new servants were recruited in the village and set to work dusting and cleaning and polishing, clearing out furniture and pulling up carpets. Their industry served only to reveal fresh requirements ; plaster mouldings, long rotten, crumbled under the feather brooms, worm-eaten mahogany floorboards came up with the tin tacks ; bare brick was disclosed behind the cabinets in the great drawing-room. A second wave of the invasion brought painters, paperhangers and plumbers, and in a moment of enthusiasm Bella had the cornice and the capitals of the pillars in the hall regilded ; windows were reglazed, banisters fitted into gaping sockets, and the stair carpet shifted so that the worn strips were less noticeable.

In all these works Bella was indefatigable. She trotted from drawing-room to hall, down the long gallery, up the staircase, admonishing the hireling servants, lending a hand with the lighter objects of furniture, sliding, when the time came, up and down the mahogany floor of the drawing-room to work in the French chalk. She unloaded chests of silver in the attics, found long-forgotten services of china, went down with Riley into the cellars to count the few remaining and now flat and acid bottles of champagne. And in the evenings when the manual labourers had retired exhausted to their gross recreations, Bella sat up far into the night turning the pages of cookery books, comparing the estimates of rival caterers, inditing long and detailed letters to the agents for dance bands and, most important of all, drawing up her list of guests and addressing the high double piles of engraved cards that stood in her escritoire.

Distance counts for little in Ireland. People will readily drive three hours to pay an afternoon call, and for a dance of such importance no journey was too great. Bella had her list painfully compiled from works of reference, Riley's more-up-to-date social knowledge and her own suddenly animated memory. Cheerfully, in a steady childish handwriting, she transferred the names to the cards and addressed the envelopes. It was the work of several late sittings. Many of those whose names were transcribed were dead or bedridden; some whom she just remembered seeing as small children were reaching retiring age in remote corners of the globe; many of the houses she wrote down were blackened shells, burned during the troubles and never rebuilt; some had "no one living in them, only farmers." But at last, none too early, the last envelope was addressed. A final lap with the stamps and then later than usual she rose from the desk. Her limbs were stiff, her eyes dazzled, her tongue cloyed with the gum of the Free State post office; she felt a little dizzy, but she locked her desk that evening with the knowledge that the most serious part of the work of the party was over. There had been severel notable and deliberate omissions from that list.

"What's all this I hear about Bella giving a party?" said Lady Gordon to Lady Mockstock. "I haven't had a card."

"Neither have I yet. I hope the old thing hasn't forgotten me. I certainly intend to go. I've never been inside the house. I believe she's got some lovely things."

With true English reserve the lady whose husband had leased Mock Hall never betrayed the knowledge that any party was in the air at all at Fleacetown.

As the last days approached Bella concentrated more upon her own appearance. She had bought few clothes of recent years, and the Dublin dressmaker with whom she used to deal had shut up shop. For a delirious instant she played with the idea of a journey to London and even Paris, and considerations of time alone obliged her to abandon it. In the end she discovered a shop to suit her, and purchased a very magnificent gown of crimson satin ; to this she added long white gloves and satin shoes. There was no tiara, alas ! among her jewels, but she unearthed large numbers of bright, nondescript Victorian rings, some chains and lockets, pearl brooches, turquoise earrings, and a collar of garnets. She ordered a coiffeur down from Dublin to dress her hair.

On the day of the ball she woke early, slightly feverish with nervous excitement, and wriggled in bed till she was called, restlessly rehearsing in her mind every detail of the arrangements. Before noon she had been to supervise the setting of hundreds of candles in the sconces round the ball-room and supper-room, and in the three great chandeliers of cut Waterford

199

glass; she had seen the supper tables laid out with silver and glass and stood the massive wine coolers by the buffet; she had helped bank the staircase and hall with chrysanthemums. She had no luncheon that day, though Riley urged her with samples of the delicacies already arrived from the caterer's. She felt a little faint; lay down for a short time, but soon rallied to sew with her own hands the crested buttons on to the liveries of the hired servants.

The invitations were timed for eight o'clock. She wondered whether that were too early —she had heard tales of parties that began very late—but as the afternoon dragged on unendurably, and rich twilight enveloped the house, Bella became glad that she had set a short term on this exhausting wait.

At six she went up to dress. The hairdresser was there with a bag full of tongs and combs. He brushed and coiled her hair and whiffed it up and generally manipulated it until it became orderly and formal and apparently far more copious. She put on all her jewellery and, standing before the cheval glass in her room, could not forbear a gasp of surprise. Then she limped downstairs.

The house looked magnificent in the candlelight. The band was there, the twelve hired

footmen, Riley in knee breeches and black silk
stockings.

It struck eight. Bella waited. Nobody
came.

She sat down on a gilt chair at the head of
the stairs, looked steadily before her with her
blank, blue eyes. In the hall, in the cloakroom,
in the supper-room, the hired footmen looked
at one another with knowing winks. " What
does the old girl expect ? No one'll have
finished dinner before ten."

The linkmen on the steps stamped and chafed
their hands.

At half-past twelve Bella rose from her chair.
Her face gave no indication of what she was
thinking.

" Riley, I think I will have some supper. I
am not feeling altogether well."

She hobbled slowly to the dining-room.

" Give me a stuffed quail and a glass of wine.
Tell the band to start playing."

The *Blue Danube* waltz flooded the house.
Bella smiled approval and swayed her head a
little to the rhythm.

" Riley, I am really quite hungry. I've had
nothing all day. Give me another quail and
some more champagne."

Alone among the candles and the hired foot-men, Riley served his mistress with an immense supper. She enjoyed every mouthful.

Presently she rose. " I am afraid there must be some mistake. No one seems to be coming to the ball. It is very disappointing after all our trouble. You may tell the band to go home."

But just as she was leaving the dining-room there was a stir in the hall. Guests were arriving. With wild resolution Bella swung herself up the stairs. She must get to the top before the guests were announced. One hand on the banister, one on her stick, pounding heart, two steps at a time. At last she reached the landing and turned to face the company. There was a mist before her eyes and a singing in her ears. She breathed with effort, but dimly she saw four figures advancing and saw Riley meet them and heard him announce

" Lord and Lady Mockstock, Sir Samuel and Lady Gordon."

Suddenly the daze in which she had been moving cleared. Here on the stairs were the two women she had not invited—Lady Mock-stock the draper's daughter, Lady Gordon the American.

She drew herself up and fixed them with her blank, blue eyes.

" I had not expected this honour," she said.

" Please forgive me if I am unable to entertain you."

The Mockstocks and the Gordons stood aghast ; saw the mad blue eyes of their hostess, her crimson dress ; the ball-room beyond, looking immense in its emptiness ; heard the dance music echoing through the empty house. The air was charged with the scent of chrysan-themums. And then the drama and unreality of the scene were dispelled. Miss Fleace suddenly sat down, and holding out her hands to her butler, said, " I don't quite know what's happening."

He and two of the hired footmen carried the old lady to a sofa. She spoke only once more. Her mind was still on the same subject. " They came uninvited, those two . . . and nobody else."

A day later she died.

Mr. Banks arrived for the funeral and spent a week sorting out her effects. Among them he found in her escritoire, stamped, addressed, but unposted, the invitations to the ball.

WINNER TAKES ALL

I

WHEN Mrs. Kent-Cumberland's eldest
son was born (in an expensive London
nursing home) there was a bonfire on
Tomb Beacon; it consumed three barrels of
tar, an immense catafalque of timber, and, as
things turned out—for the flames spread briskly
in the dry gorse and loyal tenantry were too
tipsy to extinguish them—the entire vegetation
of Tomb Hill.

As soon as mother and child could be moved,
they travelled in state to the country, where
flags were hung out in the village street and a
trellis arch of evergreen boughs obscured the
handsome Palladium entrance gates of their
home. There were farmers' dinners both at
Tomb and on the Kent-Cumberlands' Norfolk
estate, and funds for a silver-plated tray were
ungrudgingly subscribed.

The christening was celebrated by a garden-
party. A princess stood Godmother by proxy,
and the boy was called Gervase Peregrine
Mountjoy St. Eustace—all of them names
illustrious in the family's history.

207

Throughout the service and the subsequent presentations he maintained an attitude of phlegmatic dignity which confirmed everyone in the high estimate they had already formed of his capabilities.

After the garden-party there were fireworks and after the fireworks a very hard week for the gardeners, cleaning up the mess. The life of the Kent-Cumberlands then resumed its normal tranquillity until nearly two years later, when, much to her annoyance, Mrs. Kent-Cumberland discovered that she was to have another baby.

The second child was born in August in a shoddy modern house on the East Coast which had been taken for the summer so that Gervase might have the benefit of sea air. Mrs. Kent-Cumberland was attended by the local doctor, who antagonised her by his middle-class accent, and proved, when it came to the point, a great deal more deft than the London specialist.

Throughout the peevish months of waiting Mrs. Kent-Cumberland had fortified herself with the hope that she would have a daughter. It would be a softening influence for Gervase, who was growing up somewhat unresponsive, to have a pretty, gentle, sympathetic sister two years younger than himself. She would come out just when he was going up to Oxford and would save him from either of the dreadful extremes of evil company which threatened that stage of development—the bookworm and the hooligan. She would bring down delightful girls for Eights Week and Commem. Mrs. Kent-Cumberland had it all planned out. When she was delivered of another son she named him Thomas, and fretted through her convalescence with her mind on the coming hunting season.

2

The two brothers developed into sturdy, unremarkable little boys; there was little to choose between them except their two years' difference in age. They were both sandy-haired, courageous, and well-mannered on occasions. Neither was sensitive, artistic, highly strung, or conscious of being misunderstood. Both accepted the fact of Gervase's importance just as they accepted his superiority of knowledge and physique. Mrs. Kent-Cumberland was a fair-minded woman, and in the event of the two being involved in mischief, it was Gervase, as the elder, who was the more severely punished. Tom found that his obscurity was on the whole advantageous, for it

excused him from the countless minor per-
formances of ceremony which fell on Gervase.

3

At the age of seven Tom was consumed with
desire for a model motor-car, an expensive toy
of a size to sit in and pedal about the garden.
He prayed for it steadfastly every evening
and most mornings for several weeks. Christmas was approaching.

Gervase had a smart pony and was often
taken hunting. Tom was alone most of the
day and the motor-car occupied a great part
of his thoughts. Finally he confided his
ambition to an uncle. This uncle was not
addicted to expensive present giving, least of
all to children (for he was a man of limited
means and self-indulgent habits) but something
in his nephew's intensity of feeling impressed
him.

" Poor little beggar," he reflected, " his
brother seems to get all the fun," and when
he returned to London he ordered the motor-
car for Tom. It arrived some days before
Christmas and was put away upstairs with
other presents. On Christmas Eve Mrs.
Kent-Cumberland came to inspect them.

"How very kind," she said, looking at each label in turn, "how very kind."

The motor-car was by far the largest exhibit. It was pillar-box red, complete with electric lights, a hooter and a spare wheel.

"Really," she said. "How *very* kind of Ted."

Then she looked at the label more closely. "But how foolish of him. He's put *Tom's* name on it."

"There was this book for Master Gervase," said the nurse, producing a volume labelled "Gervase with best wishes from Uncle Ted."

"Of course the parcels have been confused at the shop," said Mrs. Kent-Cumberland. "This can't have been meant for Tom. Why, it must have cost six or seven pounds."

She changed the labels and went downstairs to supervise the decoration of the Christmas tree, glad to have rectified an obvious error of justice.

Next morning the presents were revealed. "Oh, Ger. You *are* lucky," said Tom, inspecting the motor-car. "May I ride in it?"

"Yes, only be careful. Nanny says it was awfully expensive."

Tom rode it twice round the room. "May I take it in the garden sometimes?"

"Yes. You can have it when I'm hunting."

Later in the week they wrote to thank their uncle for his presents.

Gervase wrote: "*Dear Uncle Ted, Thank you for the lovely present. It's lovely. The pony is very well. I am going to hunt again before I go back to school. Love from Gervase.*"

"*Dear Uncle Ted,*" wrote Tom, "*Thank you ever so much for the lovely present. It is just what I wanted. Again thanking you very much. With love from Tom.*"

"So that's all the thanks I get. Ungrateful little beggar," said Uncle Ted, resolving to be more economical in future.

But when Gervase went back to school, he said, "You can have the motor-car, Tom, to keep."

"What, for *my own* ?"

"Yes. It's a kid's toy, anyway."

And by this act of generosity he increased Tom's respect and love for him a hundredfold.

4

The War came and profoundly changed the lives of the two boys. It engendered none of the neuroses threatened by pacifists. Air raids remained among Tom's happiest memories, when the school used to be awakened in the middle of the night and hustled downstairs to the basements where, wrapped in eiderdowns, they were regaled with cocoa and cake by the matron, who looked supremely ridiculous in a flannel nightgown. Once a Zeppelin was hit in sight of the school ; they all crowded to the dormitory windows to see it sinking slowly in a globe of pink flame. A very young master whose health rendered him unfit for military service danced on the headmaster's tennis court crying, " There go the baby killers." Tom made a collection of " War Relics ", including a captured German helmet, shell-splinters, *The Times* for August 4th, 1914, buttons, cartridge cases, and cap badges, that was voted the best in the school.

The event which radically changed the relationship of the brothers was the death, early in 1915, of their father. Neither knew him well nor particularly liked him. He had represented the division in the House of Commons and spent much of his time in London while the children were at Tomb. They only saw him on three occasions after he joined the army. Gervase and Tom were called out of the class-room and told of his death by the head-master's wife. They cried, since it was expected of them, and for some days were treated with marked deference by the masters and the rest of the school.

It was in the subsequent holidays that the importance of the change became apparent. Mrs. Kent-Cumberland had suddenly become more emotional and more parsimonious. She was liable to unprecedented outbursts of tears, when she would crush Gervase to her and say, " My poor fatherless boy." At other times she spoke gloomily of death duties.

5

For some years in fact " Death Duties " became the refrain of the household.

When Mrs. Kent-Cumberland let the house in London and closed down a wing at Tomb, when she reduced the servants to four and the gardeners to two, when she " let the flower gardens go," when she stopped asking her brother Ted to stay, when she emptied the stables, and became almost fanatical in her reluctance to use the car, when the bath-water was cold and there were no new tennis-balls, when the chimneys were dirty and the lawns covered with sheep, when Gervase's cast-off clothes ceased to fit Tom, when she refused him the " extra " expense at school of carpentry lessons and mid-morning milk—" Death Duties " were responsible.

" It is all for Gervase," Mrs. Kent-Cumberland used to explain. "When he inherits, he must take over free of debt, as his father did."

6

Gervase went to Eton in the year of his father's death. Tom would normally have followed him two years later, but in her new mood of economy, Mrs. Kent-Cumberland cancelled his entry and began canvassing her friends' opinions about the less famous, cheaper public schools. "The education is just as good," she said, "and far more suitable for a boy who has his own way to make in the world."

Tom was happy enough at the school to which he was sent. It was very bleak and very new, salubrious, progressive, prosperous in the boom that secondary education enjoyed in the years immediately following the war, and, when all was said and done, "thoroughly suitable for a boy with his own way to make in the world." He had several friends whom he was not allowed to invite to his home during the holidays. He got his House colours for swimming and fives, played once or twice in the second eleven for cricket, and was a platoon-commander in the O.T.C.; he was in the sixth form and passed the Higher

Certificate in his last year, became a prefect and enjoyed the confidence of his house master, who spoke of him as "a very decent stamp of boy." He left school at the age of eighteen without the smallest desire to revisit it or see any of its members again.

Gervase was then at Christ Church. Tom went up to visit him, but the magnificent Etonians who romped in and out of his brother's rooms scared and depressed him. Gervase was in the Bullingdon, spending money freely and enjoying himself. He gave a dinner-party in his rooms, but Tom sat in silence, drinking heavily to hide his embarrassment, and was later sombrely sick in a corner of Peckwater quad. He returned to Tomb next day in the lowest spirits.

" It is not as though Tom were a scholarly boy," said Mrs. Kent-Cumberland to her friends. " I am glad he is not, of course. But if he had been, it might have been right to make the sacrifice and send him to the University. As it is, the sooner he Gets Started the better."

7

Getting Tom started, however, proved a matter of some difficulty. During the Death

Duty Period, Mrs. Kent-Cumberland had cut herself off from many of her friends. Now she cast round vainly to find someone who would "put Tom into something." Chartered Accountancy, Chinese Customs, estate agencies, "the City," were suggested and abandoned. "The trouble is, that he has no particular abilities," she explained. "He is the sort of boy who would be useful in anything —an all-round man—but, of course, he has no capital."

August, September, October passed; Gervase was back at Oxford, in fashionable lodgings in the High Street, but Tom remained at home without employment. Day by day he and his mother sat down together to luncheon and dinner, and his constant presence was a severe strain on Mrs. Kent-Cumberland's equability. She herself was always busy and, as she bustled about her duties, it shocked and distracted her to encounter the large figure of her younger son sprawling on the morning-room sofa or leaning against the stone parapet of the terrace and gazing out apathetically across the familiar landscape.

"Why can't you find something to *do* ?" she would complain. "There are *always*

things to do about a house. Heaven knows
I never have a moment." And when, one
afternoon, he was asked out by some neighbours and returned too late to dress for dinner,
she said, " Really, Tom, I should have thought
that *you* had time for that."

" It is a very serious thing," she remarked
on another occasion, " for a young man of your
age to get out of the habit of work. It saps
his whole moral."

Accordingly she fell back upon the ancient
country house expedient of Cataloguing the
Library. This consisted of an extensive and
dusty collection of books amassed by succeeding
generations of a family at no time notable for
their patronage of literature; it had been
catalogued before, in the middle of the nine-
teenth century, in the spidery, spinsterish
hand of a relative in reduced circumstances;
since then the additions and disturbances had
been negligible, but Mrs. Kent-Cumberland
purchased a fumed oak cabinet and several
boxes of cards and instructed Tom how she
wanted the shelves renumbered and the books
twice entered under Subject and Author.

It was a system that should keep a boy
employed for some time, and it was with

vexation, therefore, that, a few days after the task was commenced, she paid a surprise visit to the scene of his labour and found Tom sitting, almost lying, in an armchair, with his feet on a rung of the library steps, reading.

" I am glad you have found something interesting," she said in a voice that conveyed very little gladness.

" Well, to tell you the truth, I think I have," said Tom, and showed her the book.

It was the manuscript journal kept by a Colonel Jasper Cumberland during the Peninsular War. It had no startling literary merit, nor did its criticisms of the general staff throw any new light upon the strategy of the campaign, but it was a lively, direct, day-to-day narrative, redolent of its period ; there was a sprinkling of droll anecdotes, some vigorous descriptions of fox-hunting behind the lines of Torres Vedras, of the Duke of Wellington dining in Mess, of a threatened mutiny that had not yet found its way into history, of the assault on Badajos ; there were some bawdy references to Portuguese women and some pious reflections about patriotism.

" I was wondering if it might be worth publishing," said Tom.

" I should hardly think so," replied his

mother. "But I will certainly show it to Gervase when he comes home."

For the moment the discovery gave a new interest to Tom's life. He read up the history of the period and of his own family. Jasper Cumberland he established as a younger son of the period, who had later emigrated to Canada. There were letters from him among the archives, including the announcement of his marriage to a Papist which had clearly severed the link with his elder brother. In a case of uncatalogued miniatures in the long drawing-room, he found the portrait of a handsome whiskered soldier, which by a study of contemporary uniforms he was able to identify as the diarist.

Presently, in his round, immature handwriting, Tom began working up his notes into an essay. His mother watched his efforts with unqualified approval. She was glad to see him busy, and glad to see him taking an interest in his family's history. She had begun to fear that by sending him to a school without "tradition" she might have made a socialist of the boy. When, shortly before the Christmas vacation, work was found for Tom she took charge of his notes. "I am sure Gervase will be extremely interested," she said. "He may even think it worth showing to a publisher."

8

The work that had been found for Tom was not immediately lucrative, but, as his mother said, it was a Beginning. It was to go to Wolverhampton and learn the motor business from the bottom. The first two years were to be spent at the works, from where, if he showed talent, he might graduate to the London show-rooms. His wages, at first, were thirty-five shillings a week. This was augmented by the allowance of another pound. Lodgings were found for him over a fruit shop in the outskirts of the town, and Gervase gave him his old two-seater car, in which he could travel to and from his work, and for occasional week-ends home.

It was during one of these visits that Gervase told him the good news that a London publisher had read the diary and seen possibilities in it. Six months later it appeared under the title *The Journal of an English Cavalry Officer during the Peninsular War. Edited with notes and a biographical introduction by Gervase Kent-Cumberland*. The miniature portrait was prettily reproduced as a frontispiece, there was a collotype copy of a page of the original manuscript, a contemporary print of Tomb Park, and a map of the campaign. It sold nearly two thousand copies at twelve-and-six-pence and received two or three respectful reviews in the Saturday and Sunday papers.

The appearance of the *Journal* coincided within a few days with Gervase's twenty-first birthday. The celebrations were extravagant and prolonged, culminating in a ball at which Tom's attendance was required.

He drove over, after the works had shut down, and arrived, just in time for dinner, to find a house-party of thirty and a house entirely transformed.

His own room had been taken for a guest (" as you will only be here for one night," his mother explained). He was sent down to the Cumberland Arms, where he dressed by candle-light in a breathless little bedroom over the bar, and arrived late and slightly dishevelled at dinner, where he sat between two lovely girls who neither knew who he was nor troubled to inquire. The dancing, afterwards, was in a marquee built on the terrace, which a London catering firm had converted into a fair replica of a Pont Street drawing-room. Tom danced once or twice with the daughters of neigh-bouring families whom he had known since childhood. They asked him about Wolver-

hampton and the works. He had to get up
early next morning ; at midnight he slipped
away to his bed at the inn. The evening had
bored him ; because he was in love.

9

It had occurred to him to ask his mother
whether he might bring his fiancée to the ball,
but on reflection, enchanted as he was, he had
realised that it would not do. The girl was
named Gladys Cruttwell. She was two years
older than himself ; she had fluffy, yellow hair
which she washed at home once a week and
dried before the gas-fire ; on the day after the
shampoo it was very light and silky ; towards
the end of the week, darker and slightly greasy.
She was a virtuous, affectionate, self-reliant,
even-tempered, unintelligent, high-spirited girl,
but Tom could not disguise from himself the
fact that she would not go down well at Tomb.
    She worked for the firm on the clerical side.
Tom had noticed her on his second day, as she
tripped across the yard, exactly on time, bare-
headed (the day after a shampoo) in a woollen
coat and skirt which she had knitted herself.
He had got into conversation with her in the
canteen, by making way for her at the counter

with a chivalry that was not much practised at the works. His possession of a car gave him a clear advantage over the other young men about the place.

They discovered that they lived within a few streets of one another, and it presently became Tom's practice to call for her in the mornings and take her home in the evenings. He would sit in the two-seater outside her gate, sound the horn, and she would come running down the path to greet him. As summer approached they went for drives in the evening among leafy Warwickshire lanes. In June they were engaged. Tom was exhilarated, sometimes almost dizzy at the experience, but he hesitated to tell his mother. " After all," he reflected, " it is not as though I were Gervase," but in his own heart he knew that there would be trouble.

Gladys came of a class accustomed to long engagements; marriage seemed a remote prospect; an engagement to her signified the formal recognition that she and Tom spent their spare time in one another's company. Her mother, with whom she lived, accepted him on these terms. In years to come, when Tom had got his place in the London show-rooms, it would be time enough to think about marrying. But Tom was born to a less patient tradition.

He began to speak about a wedding in the autumn.

" It would be lovely," said Gladys in the tones she would have employed about winning the Irish sweepstake.

He had spoken very little about his family. She understood, vaguely, that they lived in a big house, but it was a part of life that never had been real to her. She knew that there were Duchesses and Marchionesses in something called " Society " ; they were encountered in the papers and the films. She knew there were directors with large salaries ; but the fact that there were people like Gervase or Mrs. Kent-Cumberland, and that they could think of themselves as radically different from herself, had not entered her experience. When, eventually, they were brought together Mrs. Kent-Cumberland was extremely gracious and Gladys thought her a very nice old lady. But Tom knew that the meeting was proving disastrous.

" Of course," said Mrs. Kent-Cumberland, " the whole thing is quite impossible. Miss What-ever-her-name-was seemed a thoroughly nice girl, but you are not in a position to think of marriage. Besides," she added with absolute finality, " you must not forget that if anything were to happen to Gervase, you would be his heir."

So Tom was removed from the motor business and an opening found for him on a sheep farm in South Australia.

10

It would not be fair to say that in the ensuing two years Mrs. Kent-Cumberland forgot her younger son. She wrote to him every month and sent him bandana handkerchiefs for Christmas. In the first, lonely days he wrote to her frequently, but when, as he grew accustomed to the new life, his letters became less frequent she did not seriously miss them. When they did arrive they were lengthy; she put them aside from her correspondence to read at leisure and, more than once, mislaid them, unopened. But whenever her acquaintances asked after Tom, she loyally answered, "Doing splendidly. And enjoying himself *very* much."

She had many other things to occupy and, in some cases, distress her. Gervase was now in authority at Tomb, and the careful régime of his minority wholly reversed. There were six expensive hunters in the stable. The lawns were mown, bedrooms thrown open, additional bathrooms installed; there was even talk of constructing a swimming-pool. There was constant Saturday to Monday entertaining. There was the sale, at a poor price, of two Romneys and a Hoppner.

Mrs. Kent-Cumberland watched all this with mingled pride and anxiety. In particular she scrutinised the succession of girls who came to stay, in the irreconcilable, ever present fears that Gervase would or would not marry. Either conclusion seemed perilous ; a wife for Gervase must be well-born, well-conducted, rich, of stainless reputation, and affectionately disposed to Mrs. Kent-Cumberland ; such a mate seemed difficult to find. The estate was clear of the mortgages necessitated by death duties, but dividends were uncertain, and though, as she frequently pointed out, she " never interfered ", simple arithmetic and her own close experience of domestic management convinced her that Gervase would not long be able to support the scale of living which he had introduced.

With so much on her mind, it was inevitable that Mrs. Kent-Cumberland should think a great deal about Tomb and very little about South Australia, and should be rudely shocked to read in one of Tom's letters that he was proposing to return to England on a visit, with a fiancée and a future father-in-law ; that in fact he had already started, was now on the sea and due to arrive in London in a fortnight. Had she read his earlier letters with attention she might have found hints of such an attachment, but she had not done so, and the announcement came to her as a wholly unpleasant surprise.

"Your brother is coming back."

"Oh, good ! When ? "

"He is bringing a farmer's daughter to whom he is engaged—and the farmer. They want to come here."

"I say, that's rather a bore. Let's tell them we're having the boilers cleaned."

"You don't seem to realise that this is a serious matter, Gervase."

"Oh, well, you fix things up. I dare say it would be all right if they came next month. We've got to have the Anchorages some time. We might get both over together."

In the end it was decided that Gervase should meet the immigrants in London, vet them and report to his mother whether or no they were suitable fellow-guests for the Anchorages. A week later, on his return to Tomb, his mother greeted him anxiously.

"Well ? You never wrote ? "

"Wrote, why should I ? I never do. I say, I haven't forgotten a birthday or anything, have I ? "

" Don't be absurd, Gervase. I mean, about your brother Tom's unfortunate entanglement. Did you see the girl ? "

" Oh, *that*. Yes, I went and had dinner with them. Tom's done himself quite well. Fair, rather fat, saucer eyed, good tempered I should say by her looks."

" Does she—does she speak with an Australian accent ? "

" Didn't notice it."

" And the father ? "

" Pompous old boy."

" Would he be all right with the Anchorages ? "

" I should think he'd go down like a dinner. But they can't come. They are staying with the Chasms."

" Indeed ! What an extraordinary thing. But, of course, Archie Chasm was Governor-General once. Still, it shows they must be fairly respectable. Where are they staying ? "

" Claridges."

" Then they must be quite rich, too. How very interesting. I will write this evening."

II

Three weeks later they arrived. Mr. MacDougal, the father, was a tall, lean man, with pince-nez and an interest in statistics. He was a territorial magnate to whom the Tomb estates appeared a cosy small-holding. He did not emphasise this in any boastful fashion, but in his statistical zeal gave Mrs. Kent-Cumberland some staggering figures. "Is Bessie your only child?" asked Mrs. Kent-Cumberland.

"My only child and heir," he replied, coming down to brass tacks at once. "I dare say you have been wondering what sort of settlement I shall be able to make on her. Now that, I regret to say, is a question I cannot answer accurately. We have good years, Mrs. Kent-Cumberland, and we have bad years. It all depends."

"But I dare say that even in bad years the income is quite considerable?"

"In a bad year," said Mr. MacDougal, "in a *very* bad year such as the present, the net profits, after all deductions have been made for running expenses, insurance, taxation, and deterioration, amount to something between" — Mrs. Kent-Cumberland listened breathlessly—"fifty and fifty-two thousand pounds. I know that is a very vague statement, but it is impossible to be more accurate until the last returns are in."

Bessie was bland and creamy. She admired everything. "It's so *antique*," she would remark with relish, whether the object of her attention was the Norman Church of Tomb, the Victorian panelling in the billiard-room, or the central-heating system which Gervase had recently installed. Mrs. Kent-Cumberland took a great liking to the girl.

"Thoroughly Teachable," she pronounced. "But I wonder whether she is *really* suited to Tom . . . I *wonder* . . ."

The MacDougals stayed for four days and, when they left, Mrs. Kent-Cumberland pressed them to return for a longer visit. Bessie had been enchanted with everything she saw.

"I wish we could live here," she had said to Tom on her first evening, "in this dear, quaint old house,"

"Yes, darling, so do I. Of course it all belongs to Gervase, but I always look on it as my home."

"Just as we Australians look on England."

"Exactly."

She had insisted on seeing everything; the old gabled manor, once the home of the family, relegated now to the function of dower house since the present mansion was built in the eighteenth century—the house of mean proportions and inconvenient offices where Mrs. Kent-Cumberland, in her moments of depression, pictured her own, declining years ; the mill and the quarries ; the farm, which to the MacDougals seemed minute and formal as a Noah's Ark. On these expeditions it was Gervase who acted as guide. " He, of course, knows so much more about it than Tom," Mrs. Kent-Cumberland explained.

Tom, in fact, found himself very rarely alone with his fiancée. Once, when they were all together after dinner, the question of his marriage was mentioned. He asked Bessie whether, now that she had seen Tomb, she would sooner be married there, at the village church, than in London.

" Oh there is no need to decide anything hastily," Mrs. Kent-Cumberland had said, " Let Bessie look about a little first."

When the MacDougals left, it was to go to Scotland to see the castle of their ancestors. Mr. MacDougal had traced relationship with various branches of his family, had corresponded with them intermittently, and now wished to make their acquaintance.

Bessie wrote to them all at Tomb ; she wrote

daily to Tom, but in her thoughts, as she lay sleepless in the appalling bed provided for her by her distant kinsmen, she was conscious for the first time of a slight feeling of disappointment and uncertainty. In Australia Tom had seemed so different from everyone else, so gentle and dignified and cultured. Here in England he seemed to recede into obscurity. Everyone in England seemed to be like Tom.

And then there was the house. It was exactly the kind of house which she had always imagined English people to live in, with the dear little park—less than a thousand acres—and the soft grass and the old stone. Tom had fitted into the house. He had fitted too well; had disappeared entirely in it and become part of the background. The central place belonged to Gervase—so like Tom but more handsome; with all Tom's charm but with more personality. Beset with these thoughts, she rolled on the hard and irregular bed until dawn began to show through the lancet window of the Victorian-baronial turret. She loved that turret for all its discomfort. It was so antique.

12

Mrs. Kent-Cumberland was an active woman. It was less than ten days after the MacDougals'

visit that she returned triumphantly from a day
in London. After dinner, when she sat alone
with Tom in the small drawing-room, she
said :

" You'll be very much surprised to hear who
I saw to-day. *Gladys*."

" Gladys ? "

" Gladys Cruttwell."

" Good heavens. Where on earth did you
meet her ? "

" It was quite by chance," said his mother
vaguely. " She is working there now."

" How was she ? "

" Very pretty. Prettier, if anything."

There was a pause. Mrs. Kent-Cumberland
stitched away at a gros-point chair seat. " You
know, dear boy, that *I never interfere*, but I have
often wondered whether you treated Gladys
very kindly. I know I was partly to blame,
myself. But you were both very young and
your prospects so uncertain. I thought a year
or two of separation would be a good test of
whether you really loved one another."

" Oh, I am sure she has forgotten about me
long ago."

" Indeed, she has not, Tom. I thought she
seemed a very unhappy girl."

" But how *can* you know, Mother, just seeing
her casually like that ? "

234

"We had luncheon together," said Mrs. Kent-Cumberland. "In an A.B.C. shop."

Another pause.

"But, look here, I've forgotten all about her. I only care about Bessie now."

"You know, dearest boy, I never interfere. I think Bessie is a delightful girl. But are you free? Are you free in your own conscience? You know, and I do not know, on what terms you parted from Gladys."

And there returned, after a long absence, the scene which for the first few months of his Australian venture had been constantly in Tom's memory, of a tearful parting and many intemperate promises. He said nothing. "I did not tell Gladys of your engagement. I thought you had the right to do that—as best you can, in your own way. But I did tell her you were back in England and that you wished to see her. She is coming here to-morrow for a night or two. She looked in need of a holiday, poor child."

When Tom went to meet Gladys at the station they stood for some minutes on the platform not certain of the other's identity. Then their tentative signs of recognition corresponded. Gladys had been engaged twice in the past two years, and was now walking out with a motor salesman. It had been a great surprise when Mrs. Kent-Cumberland sought her out and explained that Tom had returned to England. She had not forgotten him, for she was a loyal and good-hearted girl, but she was embarrassed and touched to learn that his devotion was unshaken.

They were married two weeks later and Mrs. Kent-Cumberland undertook the delicate mission of " explaining everything " to the MacDougals.

They went to Australia, where Mr. Mac-Dougal very magnanimously gave them a post managing one of his more remote estates. He was satisfied with Tom's work. Gladys has a large sunny bungalow and a landscape of grazing-land and wire fences. She does not see very much company nor does she particularly like what she does see. The neighbouring ranchers find her very English and aloof.

Bessie and Gervase were married after six weeks' engagement. They live at Tomb. Bessie has two children and Gervase has six race-horses. Mrs. Kent-Cumberland lives in the house with them. She and Bessie rarely disagree, and, when they do, it is Mrs. Kent-Cumberland who gets her way.

The dower house is let on a long lease to a sporting manufacturer. Gervase has taken over the Hounds and spends money profusely; everyone in the neighbourhood is content.

CHARLES RYDER'S SCHOOLDAYS

I

THERE WAS a scent of dust in the air ; a thin vestige surviving in the twilight from the golden clouds with which before chapel the House Room fags had filled the evening sunshine. Light was failing. Beyond the trefoils and branched mullions of the windows the towering autumnal leaf was now flat and colourless. All the eastward slope of Spierpoint Down, where the College buildings stood, lay lost in shadow ; above and behind, on the high lines of Chanctonbury and Spierpoint Ring, the first day of term was gently dying.

In the House Room thirty heads were bent over their books. Few form-masters had set any preparation that day. The Classical Upper Fifth, Charles Ryder's new form, were " revising last term's work " and Charles was writing his diary under cover of Hassall's *History*. He looked up from the page to the darkling texts which ran in Gothic script around the frieze. " *Qui diligit Deum diligit et fratrem suum.* "

" Get on with your work, Ryder," said Apthorpe.

Apthorpe has greased into being a house-captain this term, Charles wrote. *This is his first Evening School. He is being thoroughly officious and on his dignity.*

" Can we have the light on, please ? "

" All right. Wykham-Blake, put it on." A small boy rose from the under-school table. " Wykham-Blake, I said. There's no need for everyone to move."

A rattle of the chain, a hiss of gas, a brilliant white light over half the room. The other light hung over the new boys' table.

" Put the light on, one of you, whatever your names are."

Six startled little boys looked at Apthorpe and at one another, all began to rise together, all sat down, all looked at Apthorpe in consternation.

" Oh, for heaven's sake."

Apthorpe leaned over their heads and pulled the chain ; there was a hiss of gas but no light. " The bye-pass is out. Light it, you." He threw a box of matches to one of the new boys who dropped it, picked it up, climbed on the table and looked miserably at the white glass shade, the three hissing mantles and at Apthorpe. He had never seen a lamp of this kind before ; at home and at his private school there was electricity. He lit a match and poked at the lamp, at first without effect ; then there was a loud explosion ; he stepped back, stumbled and nearly lost his footing among the books and ink-pots, blushed hotly and regained the bench. The matches remained in his hand and he stared at them, lost in an agony of indecision. How should he dispose of them ? No head was raised but everyone in the House Room exulted in the drama. From the other side of the room Apthorpe held out his hand invitingly.

" When you have quite finished with my matches perhaps you'll be so kind as to give them back."

In despair the new boy threw them towards the house-captain; in despair he threw slightly wide. Apthorpe made no attempt to catch them, but watched them curiously as they fell to the floor. " How very extraordinary," he said. The new boy looked at the match-box ; Apthorpe looked at the new boy. " Would it be troubling you too much if I asked you to give me my matches ? " he said.

The new boy rose to his feet, walked the few steps, picked up the match-box and gave it to the house-captain, with the ghastly semblance of a smile.

" Extraordinary crew of new men we have this term," said Apthorpe. " They seem to be entirely half-witted. Has anyone been turned on to look after this man ? "

" Please, I have," said Wykham-Blake.

" A grave responsibility for one so young. Try and convey to his limited intelligence that it may prove a painful practice here to throw match-boxes about in Evening School, and laugh at house officials. By the way, is that a work-book you're reading ? "

" Oh, yes, Apthorpe." Wykham-Blake raised a face of cherubic innocence and presented the back of the *Golden Treasury*.

" Who's it for ? "

" Mr. Graves. We're to learn any poem we like."

" And what have you chosen ? "

" Milton-on-his-blindness."

" How, may one ask, did that take your fancy ? "

" I learned it once before," said Wykham-Blake and Apthorpe laughed indulgently.

" Young blighter," he said.

Charles wrote: *Now he is snooping round seeing what books men are reading. It would be typical if he got someone beaten his first Evening School. The day before yesterday this time I was in my dinner-jacket just setting out for dinner at the d'Italie with Aunt Philippa before going to* The Choice *at Wyndhams.*

Quantum mutatus ab illo Hectore. *We live in water-tight compartments. Now I am absorbed in the trivial round of House politics. Graves has played hell with the house. Apthorpe a house-captain and O'Malley on the Settle. The only consolation was seeing the woe on Wheatley's fat face when the locker list went up. He thought he was a cert for the Settle this term. Bad luck on Tamplin though. I never expected to get on but I ought by all rights to have been above O'Malley. What a tick Graves is. It all comes of this rotten system of switching round house-tutors. We ought to have the best of Heads instead of which they try out ticks like Graves on us before giving them a house. If only we still had Frank.*

Charles's handwriting had lately begun to develop certain ornamental features—Greek E's and flourished crossings. He wrote with conscious style. Whenever Apthorpe came past he would turn a page in the history book, hesitate and then write as though making a note from the text. The hands of the clock crept on to half past seven when the porter's handbell began to sound in the cloisters on the far side of Lower Quad. This was the signal of release. Throughout the House Room heads were raised, pages blotted, books closed, fountain-pens screwed up. " Get on with your work," said

Apthorpe; "I haven't said anything about moving." The porter and his bell passed up the cloisters, grew faint under the arch by the library steps, were barely audible in the Upper Quad, grew louder on the steps of Old's House and very loud in the cloister outside Head's. At last Apthorpe tossed the *Bystander* on the table and said "All right."

The House Room rose noisily. Charles underlined the date at the head of his page—*Wednesday Sept. 24th, 1919*—blotted it and put the note-book in his locker. Then with his hands in his pockets he followed the crowd into the dusk.

To keep his hands in his pockets thus—with his coat back and the middle button alone fastened—was now his privilege, for he was in his third year. He could also wear coloured socks and was indeed at the moment wearing a pair of heliotrope silk with white clocks, purchased the day before in Jermyn Street. There were several things, formerly forbidden, which were now his right. He could link his arm in a friend's and he did so now, strolling across to Hall arm-in-arm with Tamplin.

They paused at the top of the steps and stared out in the gloaming. To their left the great bulk of the chapel loomed immensely; below them the land fell away in terraces to the playing-fields with their dark fringe of elm ; head-lights moved continuously up and down the coast road; the estuary was just traceable, a lighter streak across the grey lowland, before it merged into the calm and invisible sea.

" Same old view," said Tamplin.

" Give me the lights of London," said Charles. " I say, it's rotten luck for you about the Settle."

" Oh, I never had a chance. It's rotten luck on *you*."

" Oh, I never had a chance. But *O'Malley*."

" It all comes of having that tick Graves instead of Frank."

" The buxom Wheatley looked jolly bored. Anyway, I don't envy O'Malley's job as head of the dormitory."

" That's how he got on the Settle. Tell you later."

From the moment they reached the Hall steps they had to unlink their arms, take their hands out of their pockets and stop talking. When Grace had been said Tamplin took up the story.

" Graves had him in at the end of last term and said he was making him head of the dormitory. The head of Upper Dormitory never has been on the Settle before last term when they moved Easton up from Lower Anteroom

247

after we ragged Fletcher. O'Malley told Graves he couldn't take it unless he had an official position."

" How d'you know ? "

" O'Malley told me. He thought he'd been rather fly."

" Typical of Graves to fall for a tick like that."

" It's all very well," said Wheatley, plaintively, from across the table ; " I don't think they've any right to put Graves in like this. I only came to Spierpoint because my father knew Frank's brother in the Guards. I was jolly bored, I can tell you, when they moved Frank. I think he wrote to the Head about it. We pay more in Head's and get the worst of everything."

" Tea, please."

" Same old College tea."

" Same old College eggs."

" It always takes a week before one gets used to College food."

" I never get used to it."

" Did you go to many London restaurants in the holidays ? "

" I was only in London a week. My brother took me to lunch at the Berkeley. Wish I was there now. I had two glasses of port."

" The Berkeley's all right in the evening," said Charles, " if you want to dance."

" It's jolly well all right for luncheon. You should see their hors d'oeuvres. I reckon there were twenty or thirty things to choose from. After that we had grouse and meringues with ices in them."

" I went to dinner at the d'Italie."

" Oh, where's that ? "

" It's a little place in Soho not many people know about. My aunt speaks Italian like a native so she knows all those places. Of course, there's no marble or music. It just exists for the cooking. Literary people and artists go there. My aunt knows lots of them."

" My brother says all the men from Sandhurst go to the Berkeley. Of course, they fairly rook you."

" I always think the Berkeley's rather rowdy," said Wheatley. " We stayed at Claridges after we came back from Scotland because our flat was still being done up."

" My brother says Claridges is a deadly hole."

" Of course, it isn't everyone's taste. It's rather exclusive."

" Then how did our buxom Wheatley come to be staying there, I wonder ? "

" There's no need to be cheap, Tamplin."

"I always say," suddenly said a boy named Jorkins, "that you get the best meal in London at the Holborn Grill."

Charles, Tamplin and Wheatley turned with cold curiosity on the interrupter, united at last in their disdain. "*Do* you, Jorkins? How very original of you."

"Do you *always* say that, Jorkins? Don't you sometimes get tired of *always* saying the same thing?"

"There's a four-and-sixpenny table d'hôte."

"Please, Jorkins, spare us the hideous details of your gormandising."

"Oh, all right. I thought you were interested, that's all."

"Do you think," said Tamplin, confining himself ostentatiously to Charles and Wheatley, "that Apthorpe is keen on Wykham-Blake?"

"No, is he?"

"Well, he couldn't keep away from him in Evening School."

"I suppose the boy had to find consolation now his case Sugdon's left. He hasn't a friend among the under-schools."

"What d'you make of the man Peacock?" (Charles, Tamplin and Wheatley were all in the Classical Upper Fifth under Mr. Peacock.)

"He's started decently. No work tonight."

"Raggable?"

" I doubt it. But slack."

" I'd sooner a master were slack than rag-gable. I got quite exhausted last term ragging the Tea-cake."

" It was witty, though."

" I hope he's not so slack that we shan't get our Certificates next summer."

" One can always sweat the last term. At the University no one ever does any work until just before the exams. Then they sit up all night with black coffee and strychnine."

" It would be jolly witty if no one passed his Certificate."

" I wonder what they'd do."

" Give Peacock the push, I should think."

Presently Grace was said and the school streamed out into the cloisters. It was now dark. The cloisters were lit at intervals by gas-lamps. As one walked, one's shadow lengthened and grew fainter before one until, approaching the next source of light, it disappeared, fell behind, followed one's heels, shortened, deepened, disappeared and started again at one's toes. The quarter of an hour between Hall and Second Evening was mainly spent in walking the cloisters in pairs or in threes; to walk four abreast was the privilege of school prefects. On the steps of Hall, Charles was approached by O'Malley. He was an ungainly boy, an upstart who had come to Spierpoint late, in a bye-term. He was in Army Class B and his sole distinction was staying-power in cross-country running.

"Coming to the Graves?"

"No."

"D'you mind if I hitch on to you for a minute?"

"Not particularly."

They joined the conventional, perambulating couples, their shadows, lengthened before them, apart. Charles did not take O'Malley's arm. O'Malley might not take Charles's. The Settle was purely a House Dignity. In the cloisters Charles was senior by right of his two years at Spierpoint.

"I'm awfully sorry about the Settle," said O'Malley.

"I should have thought you'd be pleased."

"I'm not, honestly. It's the last thing I wanted. Graves sent me a postcard a week ago. It spoiled the end of the holidays. I'll tell you what happened. Graves had me in on the last day last term. You know the way he has. He said, 'I've some unpleasant news for you, O'Malley. I'm putting you head of the Upper Dormitory.' I said, 'It ought to be someone on the Settle. No one else could keep order.' I thought he'd keep Easton up there. He said,

'These things are a matter of personality, not of official position.' I said, 'It's been proved you have an official. You know how bolshie we were with Fletcher.' He said, 'Fletcher wasn't the man for the job. He wasn't my appointment.'"

"Typical of his lip. Fletcher was Frank's appointment."

"I wish we had Frank still."

"So does everyone. Anyway, why are you telling me all this?"

"I didn't want you to think I'd been greasing. I heard Tamplin say I had."

"Well, you are on the Settle and you are head of the dormitory, so what's the trouble?"

"Will you back me up, Ryder?"

"Have you ever known me back anyone up, as you call it?"

"No," said O'Malley miserably, "that's just it."

"Well, why d'you suppose I should start with you?"

"I just thought you might."

"Well, think again."

They had walked three sides of the square and were now at the door of Head's House. Mr. Graves was standing outside his own room talking to Mr. Peacock.

"Charles," he said, "come here a minute. Have you met this young man yet, Peacock? He's one of yours."

"Yes, I think so," said Mr. Peacock doubt-fully.

"He's one of my problem children. Come in here, Charles. I want to have a chat to you."

Mr. Graves took him by the elbow and led him into his room.

There were no fires yet and the two arm-chairs stood before an empty grate ; everything was unnaturally bare and neat after the holiday cleaning.

"Sit you down."

Mr. Graves filled his pipe and gave Charles a long, soft and quizzical stare. He was a man still under thirty, dressed in Lovat tweed with an Old Rugbeian tie. He had been at Spier-point during Charles's first term and they had met once on the miniature range ; in that bleak, untouchable epoch Charles had been warmed by his affability. Then Mr. Graves was called up for the army and now had returned, the term before, as House Tutor of Head's. Charles had grown confident in the meantime and felt no need of affable masters ; only for Frank whom Mr. Graves had supplanted. The ghost of Frank filled the room. Mr. Graves had hung some Medici prints in the place of Frank's foot-ball groups. The set of *Georgian Poetry* in the bookcase was his, not Frank's. His college arms embellished the tobacco jar on the chimney-piece.

" Well, Charles Ryder," said Mr. Graves at length, " are you feeling sore with me ? "

" Sir ? "

Mr. Graves became suddenly snappish. " If you choose to sit there like a stone image, I can't help you."

Still Charles said nothing.

" I have a friend," said Mr. Graves, " who goes in for illumination. I thought you might like me to show him the work you sent in to the Art Competition last term."

" I'm afraid I left it at home, sir."

" Did you do any during the holidays ? "

" One or two things, sir."

" You never try painting from nature ? "

" Never, sir."

" It seems rather a crabbed, shut-in sort of pursuit for a boy of your age. Still, that's your own business."

" Yes, sir."

" Difficult chap to talk to, aren't you, Charles ? "

" Not with everyone. Not with Frank," Charles wished to say ; " I could talk to Frank by the hour." Instead he said, " I suppose I am, sir."

" Well, I want to talk to you. I dare say

you feel you have been a little ill-used this term. Of course, all your year are in rather a difficult position. Normally there would have been seven or eight people leaving at the end of last term but with the war coming to an end they are staying on an extra year, trying for University scholarships and so on. Only Sugdon left, so instead of a general move there was only one vacancy at the top. That meant only one vacancy on the Settle. I dare say you think you ought to have had it."

" No, sir. There were two people ahead of me."

" But not O'Malley. I wonder if I can make you understand why I put him over you. You were the obvious man in many ways. The thing is, some people *need* authority, others don't. You've got plenty of personality. O'Malley isn't at all sure of himself. He might easily develop into rather a second-rater. You're in no danger of that. What's more, there's the dormitory to consider. I think I can trust you to work loyally under O'Malley. I'm not so sure I could trust him to work under you. See ? It's always been a difficult dormitory. I don't want a repetition of what happened with Fletcher. Do you understand ? "

" I understand what you mean, sir."

" Grim young devil, aren't you ? "

" Sir ? "

" Oh, all right, go away.   I shan't waste any more time with you."

" Thank you, sir."

Charles rose to go.

" I'm getting a small hand printing-press this term," said Mr. Graves.   " I thought it might interest you."

It did interest Charles intensely.   It was one of the large features of his day-dreams ; in chapel, in school, in bed, in all the rare periods of abstraction, when others thought of racing motor-cars and hunters and speed-boats, Charles thought long and often of a private press.   But he would not betray to Mr. Graves the intense surge of images that rose in his mind.

" I think the invention of movable type was a disaster, sir.   It destroyed calligraphy."

" You're a prig, Charles," said Mr. Graves. " I'm sick of you.   Go away.   Tell Wheatley I want him.   And try not to dislike me so much. It wastes both our time."

Second Evening had begun when Charles returned to the House Room ; he reported to the house-captain in charge, despatched Wheatley to Mr. Graves and settled down over his Hassall to half an hour's day-dream, imagining the tall folios, the wide margins, the deckle-edged mould-made paper, the engraved initials, the rubrics and colophons of his private press. In Third Evening one could " read "; Charles read Hugh Walpole's *Fortitude*.

Wheatley did not return until the bell was ringing for the end of Evening School.

Tamplin greeted him with " Bad luck, Wheatley. How many did you get ? Was he tight ? "; Charles with " Well, you've had a long hot-air with Graves. What on earth did he talk about ? "

" It was all rather confidential," said Wheatley solemnly.

" Oh, sorry."

" No, I'll tell *you* sometime if you promise to keep it to yourself." Together they ascended the turret stair to their dormitory. " I say, have you noticed something ? Apthorpe is in the Upper Anteroom this term. Have you ever known the junior house-captain anywhere except in the Lower Anteroom ? I wonder how he worked it."

" Why should he want to ? "

" Because, my innocent, Wykham-Blake has been moved into the Upper Anteroom."

" Tactful of Graves."

" You know, I sometimes think perhaps we've rather misjudged Graves."

" You didn't think so in Hall."

" No, but I've been thinking since."

" You mean he's been greasing up to you."

" Well, all I can say is, when he wants to be decent, he *is* decent. I find we know quite a lot of the same people in the holidays. He once stayed on the moor next to ours."

" I don't see anything particularly decent in that."

" Well, it makes a sort of link. He explained why he put O'Malley on the Settle. He's a student of character, you know."

" Who ? O'Malley ? "

" No, Graves. He said that's the only reason he is a schoolmaster."

" I expect he's a schoolmaster because it's so jolly slack."

" Not at all. As a matter of fact, he was going into the Diplomatic, just as I am."

" I don't expect he could pass the exam. It's frightfully stiff. Graves only takes the Middle Fourth."

" The exam is only to keep out undesirable types."

" Then it would floor Graves."

" He says schoolmastering is the most *human* calling in the world. Spierpoint is not an arena for competition. We have to stop the weakest going to the wall."

" Did Graves say that ? "

" Yes."

259

"I must remember that if there's any unpleasantness with Peacock. What else did he say?"

"Oh, we talked about people, you know, and their characters. Would you say O'Malley had poise?"

"Good God, no."

"That's just what Graves thinks. He says some people have it naturally and they can look after themselves. Others, like O'Malley, need bringing on. He thinks authority will give O'Malley poise."

"Well, it doesn't seem to have worked yet," said Charles, as O'Malley loped past their beds to his corner.

"Welcome to the head of the dormitory," said Tamplin. "Are we all late? Are you going to report us?"

O'Malley looked at his watch. "As a matter of fact, you have exactly seven minutes."

"Not by my watch."

"We go by mine."

"Really," said Tamplin. "Has your watch been put on the Settle, too? It looks a cheap kind of instrument to me."

"When I am speaking officially I don't want any impertinence, Tamplin."

"His watch *has* been put on the Settle. It's

the first time I ever heard one could be impertinent to a watch."

They undressed and washed their teeth. O'Malley looked repeatedly at his watch and at last said, " Say your dibs."

Everyone knelt at his bedside and buried his face in the bedclothes. After a minute, in quick succession, they rose and got into bed ; all save Tamplin who remained kneeling. O'Malley stood in the middle of the dormitory, irresolute, his hand on the chain of the gas-lamp. Three minutes passed ; it was the convention that no one spoke while anyone was still saying his prayers ; several boys began to giggle. " Hurry up," said O'Malley.

Tamplin raised a face of pained rebuke. " *Please*, O'Malley. I'm saying my dibs."

" Well, you're late."

Tamplin remained with his face buried in the blanket. O'Malley pulled the chain and extinguished the light, all save the pale glow of the bye-pass under the white enamel shade. It was the custom, when doing this, to say " Goodnight"; but Tamplin was still ostensibly in prayer ; in this black predicament O'Malley stalked to his bed in silence.

" Aren't you going to say ' Goodnight ' to us ? " asked Charles.

" Goodnight."

261

A dozen voices irregularly took up the cry. "Goodnight, O'Malley . . . I hope the official watch doesn't stop in the night . . . happy dreams, O'Malley."

"Really, you know," said Wheatley, "there's a man still saying his prayers."

"Stop talking."

"*Please*," said Tamplin, on his knees. He remained there for half a minute more, then rose and got into bed.

"You understand, Tamplin? You're late."

"Oh, but I don't think I can be, even by your watch. I was perfectly ready when you said 'Say your dibs.'"

"If you want to take as long as that you must start sooner."

"But I couldn't with all that noise going on, could I, O'Malley? All that wrangling about watches?"

"We'll talk about it in the morning."

"Goodnight, O'Malley."

At this moment the door opened and the house-captain in charge of the dormitory came in. "What the devil's all this talking about?" he asked.

Now, O'Malley had not the smallest intention of giving Tamplin a "late". It was a delicate legal point, of the kind that was debated endlessly at Spierpoint, whether in the circumstances he could properly do so. It had been in O'Malley's mind to appeal to Tamplin's better nature in the morning, to say that he could take a joke as well as the next man, that his official position was repugnant to him, that the last thing he wished to do was start the term by using his new authority on his former associates ; he would say all this and ask Tamplin to " back him up ". But now, suddenly challenged out of the darkness, he lost his head and said, " I was giving Tamplin a ' late ', Anderson."

" Well, remind me in the morning and for Christ's sake don't make such a racket over it."

" Please, Anderson, I don't think I was late," said Tamplin ; " it's just that I took longer than the others over my prayers. I was perfectly ready when we were told to say them."

" But he was still out of bed when I put the light out," said O'Malley.

" Well, it's usual to wait until everyone's ready, isn't it ? "

" Yes, Anderson. I did wait about five minutes."

" I see. Anyhow, lates count from the time you start saying your dibs. You know that. Better wash the whole thing out."

" Thank you, Anderson," said Tamplin.

The house-captain lit the candle which stood in a biscuit-box shade on the press by his bed.

He undressed slowly, washed and, without saying prayers, got into bed. Then he lay there reading. The tin hid the light from the dormitory and cast a small, yellow patch over his book and pillow ; that and the faint circle of the gas-lamp were the only lights ; gradually in the darkness the lancet windows became dimly visible. Charles lay on his back thinking ; O'Malley had made a fiasco of his first evening ; first and last he could not have done things worse ; it seemed a rough and tortuous road on which Mr. Graves had set his feet, to self-confidence and poise.

Then, as he grew sleepier, Charles's thoughts, like a roulette ball when the wheel runs slow, sought their lodging and came at last firmly to rest on that day, never far distant, at the end of his second term ; the raw and gusty day of the junior steeplechase when, shivering and half-changed, queasy with apprehension of the trial ahead, he had been summoned by Frank, had shuffled into his clothes, run headlong down the turret stairs and with a new and deeper alarm knocked at the door.

" Charles, I have just had a telegram from your father which you must read. I'll leave you alone with it."

He shed no tear, then or later ; he did not remember what was said when two minutes later Frank returned ; there was a numb, anaesthetized patch at the heart of his sorrow ; he remembered, rather, the order of the day. Instead of running he had gone down in his overcoat with Frank to watch the finish of the race ; word had gone round the house and no questions were asked ; he had tea with the matron, spent the evening in her room and slept that night in a room in the Headmaster's private house ; next morning his Aunt Philippa came and took him home. He remembered all that went on outside himself, the sight and sound and smell of the place, so that, on his return to them, they all spoke of his loss, of the sharp severance of all the bonds of childhood, and it seemed to him that it was not in the uplands of Bosnia but here at Spierpoint, on the turret stairs, in the unlighted box-room passage, in the windy cloisters, that his mother had fallen, killed not by a German shell but by the shrill voice sounding across the changing room, " Ryder here ? Ryder ? Frank wants him at the double."

2

Thursday, September 25th, 1919. Peacock began well by not turning up for early school so at five past we walked out and went back to our House Rooms and I read Fortitude *by Wal-*

pole ; it is strong meat but rather unnecessary in places. After breakfast O'Malley came greasing up to Tamplin and apologised. Everyone is against him. I maintain he was in the right until he reported him late to Anderson. No possible defence for that—sheer windiness. Peacock deigned to turn up for Double Greek. We mocked him somewhat. He is trying to make us use the new pronunciation ; when he said óú there was a wail of " ooh " and Tamplin pronounced subjunctive soobyoongteeway— very witty. Peacock got bored and said he'd report him to Graves but relented. Library was open 5–6 tonight. I went meaning to put in some time on Walter Crane's Bases of Design *but Mercer came up with that weird man in Brent's called Curtis-Dunne. I envy them having Frank as house-master. He is talking of starting a literary and artistic society for men not in the Sixth. Curtis-Dunne wants to start a political group. Pretty good lift considering this is his second term although he is sixteen and has been at Dartmouth. Mercer gave me a poem to read—very sloppy. Before this there was a House Game. Everyone puffing and blowing after the holidays. Anderson said I shall probably be centre-half in the Under Sixteens—the sweatiest place in the field. I must get into training quickly.*

Friday 26th. Corps day but quite slack. Reorganisation. I am in A Company at last. A tick in Boucher's called Spratt is platoon commander. We ragged him a bit. Wheatley is a section commander! Peacock sent Bankes out of the room in Greek Testament for saying "Who will rid me of this turbulent priest" when put on to translate. Jolly witty. He began to argue. Peacock said, "Must I throw you out by force?" Bankes began to go but muttered "Muscular Christianity." Peacock: "What did you say?"; "Nothing, sir"; "Get out before I kick you." Things got a bit duller after that. Uncle George gave Bankes three.

Saturday 27th. Things very dull in school. Luckily Peacock forgot to set any preparation. Pop. Sci. in last period. Tamplin and Mercer got some of the weights that are so precious they are kept in a glass case and picked up with tweezers, made them red hot on a bunsen burner and dropped them in cold water. A witty thing to do. House Game—Under Sixteen team against a mixed side. They have put Wykham-Blake centre-half and me in goal; a godless place. Library again. Curtis-Dunne buttonholed me again. He drawled " My father is in parliament but he is a very unenlightened conservative. I of course am a socialist. That's

267

the reason I chucked the Navy." I said, " Or did they chuck you ? " " The pangs of parting were endured by both sides with mutual stoicism." He spoke of Frank as " essentially a well-intentioned fellow." Sunday tomorrow thank God. I may be able to get on with illuminating " The Bells of Heaven ".

3

Normally on Sundays there was a choice of service. Matins at a quarter to eight or Communion at quarter past. On the first Sunday of term there was Choral Communion for all at eight o'clock.

The chapel was huge, bare, and still unfinished, one of the great monuments of the Oxford Movement and the Gothic revival. Like an iceberg it revealed only a small part of its bulk above the surface of the terraced down ; below lay a crypt and below that foundations of great depth. The Founder had chosen the site and stubbornly refused to change it so that the original estimates had been exceeded before the upper chapel was begun. Visiting preachers frequently drew a lesson from the disappointments, uncertainties and final achievement of the Founder's " vision ". Now the whole nave rose triumphantly over the surrounding landscape, immense, clustered shafts supporting the groined roof ; at the west it ended abruptly in concrete and timber and corrugated iron, while behind, in a waste land near the kitchens, where the Corps band practised their bugles in the early morning, lay a nettle-and-bramble-grown ruin, the base of a tower, twice as high as the chapel, which one day was to rise so that on stormy nights, the Founder had decreed, prayers might be sung at its summit for sailors in peril on the sea.

From outside the windows had a deep, sub-marine tinge, but from inside they were clear white, and the morning sun streamed in over the altar and the assembled school. The pre-fect in Charles's row was Symonds, editor of the Magazine, president of the Debating Society, the leading intellectual. Symonds was in Head's ; he pursued a course of lonely study, seldom taking Evening School, never playing any game except, late in the evenings of the summer term, an occasional single of lawn ten-nis, appearing rarely even in the Sixth Form, but working in private under Mr. A. A. Car-michael for the Balliol scholarship. Symonds kept a leather-bound copy of the *Greek Anthol-ogy* in his place in chapel and read it throughout the services with a finely negligent air.

The masters sat in stalls orientated between

the columns, the clergy in surplices, laymen in gowns. Some of the masters who taught the Modern Side wore hoods of the newer universities ; Major Stebbing, the adjutant of the OTC, had no gown at all; Mr. A. A. Carmichael—awfully known at Spierpoint as " A.A.", the splendid dandy and wit, fine flower of the Oxford Union and the New College Essay Society, the reviewer of works of classical scholarship for the *New Statesman,* to whom Charles had never yet spoken ; whom Charles had never yet heard speak directly, but only at third hand as his *mots,* in their idiosyncratic modulations, passed from mouth to mouth from the Sixth in sanctuary to the catechumens in the porch ; whom Charles worshipped from afar—Mr. Carmichael, from a variety of academic costume, was this morning robed as a baccalaureate of Salamanca. He looked, as he stooped over his desk, like the prosecuting counsel in a cartoon by Daumier.

Nearly opposite him across the chapel stood Frank Bates ; an unbridged gulf of boys separated these rival and contrasted deities, that one the ineffable dweller on cloud-capped Olympus, this the homely clay image, the intimate of hearth and household, the patron of threshing-floor and olive-press. Frank wore only an ermine hood, a BA's gown, and loose, unremarkable clothes, subfusc today, with the Corinthian tie which alternated with the Carthusian, week in, week out. He was a clean, curly, spare fellow ; a little wan for he was in constant pain from an injury on the football field which had left him lame and kept him at Spierpoint throughout the war. This pain of his redeemed him from heartiness. In chapel his innocent, blue eyes assumed a puzzled, rather glum expression like those of an old-fashioned child in a room full of grown-ups. Frank was a bishop's son.

Behind the masters, out of sight in the side aisles, was a dowdy huddle of matrons and wives.

The service began with a procession of the choir : " Hail Festal Day ", with Wykham-Blake as the treble cantor. At the rear of the procession came Mr. Peacock, the Chaplain and the Headmaster. A week ago Charles had gone to church in London with Aunt Philippa. He did not as a rule go to church in the holidays, but being in London for the last week Aunt Philippa had said, " There's nothing much we can do today. Let's see what entertainment the Church can offer. I'm told there is a very remarkable freak named Father Wimperis." So, together, they had gone on the top of a bus to a northern suburb where Mr. Wimperis was at the time drawing great congregations. His preaching was not theatrical by Neapolitan standards, Aunt Philippa said afterwards; "However, I enjoyed him hugely. He is irresistibly common." For twenty minutes Mr. Wimperis alternately fluted and boomed from the pulpit, wrestled with the reading-stand and summoned the country to industrial peace. At the end he performed a little ceremony of his own invention, advancing to the church steps in cope and biretta with what proved to be a large silver salt cellar in his hands. "My people," he said simply, scattering salt before him, "you are the salt of the earth."

"I believe he has something new like that every week," said Aunt Philippa. "It must be lovely to live in his neighbourhood."

Charles's was not a God-fearing home. Until August 1914 his father had been accustomed to read family prayers every morning; on the outbreak of war he abruptly stopped the practice, explaining, when asked, that there was now nothing left to pray for. When Charles's mother was killed there was a memorial service for her at Boughton, his home village, but Charles's father did not go with him and Aunt Philippa. "It was all her confounded patriotism," he said, not to Charles but to Aunt Philippa, who did not repeat the remark until many years later. "She had no business to go off to Serbia like that. Do you think it my duty to marry again ? "

" No," said Aunt Philippa.

" Nothing would induce me to—least of all my duty."

The service followed its course. As often happened, two small boys fainted and were carried out by house-captains ; a third left bleeding at the nose. Mr. Peacock sang the Gospel overloudly. It was his first public appearance. Symonds looked up from his Greek, frowned and continued reading. Presently it was time for Communion ; most of the boys who had been confirmed went up to the chancel rails, Charles with them. Symonds sat back, twisted his long legs into the aisle to allow his row to pass, and remained in his place. Charles took Communion and returned to his row. He had been confirmed the term before, incuriously, without expectation or disappointment. When, later in life, he read accounts of the emotional disturbances caused in other boys by the ceremony he found them unintelligible ; to Charles it was one of the rites of adolescence, like being made, when a new boy, to stand on the table and sing. The Chaplain had " prepared " him and had confined his conferences to theology. There had been no probing of his sexual life ; he had no sexual life to probe. Instead they had talked of prayer and the sacraments.

Spierpoint was a product of the Oxford Movement, founded with definite religious aims ; in eighty years it had grown more and more to resemble the older Public Schools, but there was still a strong ecclesiastical flavour in the place. Some boys were genuinely devout and their peculiarity was respected ; in general profanity was rare and ill-looked-on. Most of the Sixth professed themselves agnostic or atheist.

The school had been chosen for Charles because, at the age of eleven, he had had a " religious phase " and told his father that he wished to become a priest.

" Good heavens," his father said ; " or do you mean a parson ? "

" A priest of the Anglican Church," said Charles precisely.

" That's better. I thought you meant a Roman Catholic. Well, a parson's is not at all a bad life for a man with a little money of his own. They can't remove you except for flagrant immorality. Your uncle has been trying to get rid of his fellow at Boughton for ten years—a most offensive fellow but perfectly chaste. He won't budge. It's a great thing in life to have a place you can't be removed from—too few of them."

But the "phase" had passed and lingered now only in Charles's love of Gothic architecture and breviaries.

After Communion Charles sat back in his chair thinking about the secular, indeed slightly anti-clerical, lyric which, already inscribed, he was about to illuminate, while the masters and, after them, the women from the side aisles, went up to the rails.

The food on Sundays was always appreciably worse than on other days ; breakfast invariably consisted of boiled eggs, overboiled and luke-warm.

Wheatley said, " How many ties do you suppose A.A.'s got ? "

" I began counting last term," said Tamplin, " and got to thirty."

" Including bows ? "

" Yes."

" Of course, he's jolly rich."

" Why doesn't he keep a car, then ? " asked Jorkins.

The hour after breakfast was normally devoted to letter-writing, but today a railway strike had been called and there were no posts. Moreover, since it was the start of term, there was no Sunday Lesson. The whole morning was therefore free and Charles had extracted permission to spend it in the Drawing School. He collected his materials and was soon happily at work.

The poem—Ralph Hodgson's " 'Twould ring the bells of Heaven The wildest peal for years, If Parson lost his senses And people came to theirs . . ."—was one of Frank's favourites. In the happy days when he had been House Tutor of Head's, Frank had read poetry aloud on Sunday evenings to any in Head's who cared to come, which was mostly the lower half of the House. He read " There swimmeth One Who swam e'er rivers were begun, And under that Almighty Fin the littlest fish may enter in " and " Abou Ben Adhem, may his tribe increase " and " Under the wide and starry sky " and " What have I done for you, England, my England . . . ? " and many others of the same comfortable kind ; but always before the end of the evening someone would say " Please, sir, can we have ' The Bells of Heaven' ? " Now he read only to his own house but the poems, Frank's pleasant voices, his nightingales, were awake still, warm and bright with remembered firelight

Charles did not question whether the poem was not perfectly suited to the compressed thirteenth-century script in which he had written it.

His method of writing was first to draw the letters faintly, free-hand in pencil ; then with a ruler and ruling-pen to ink in the uprights firmly in Indian ink until the page consisted of lines of short and long black perpendiculars ; then with a mapping-pen he joined them with hair strokes and completed their lozenge-shaped terminals. It was a method he had evolved for himself by trial and error. The initial letters of each line were left blank and these, during the last week of the holidays, he had filled with vermilion, carefully drawn, " Old English " capitals. The *T* alone remained to do and for this he had selected a model from Shaw's *Alphabets,* now open before him on the table. It was a florid fifteenth-century letter which needed considerable ingenuity of adaption, for he had decided to attach to it the decorative tail of the *J.* He worked happily, entirely absorbed, drawing in pencil, then tensely, with breath held, inking the outline with a mapping-pen ; then, when it was dry—how often, in his impatience, he had ruined his work by attempting this too soon— rubbing away the pencil lines. Finally he got out his water colours and his red sable brushes. At heart he knew he was going too fast—a monk would take a week over a single letter—but he worked with intensity and in less than two hours the initial with its pendant, convoluted border was finished. Then, as he put away his brushes, the exhilaration left him. It was no good ; it was botched ; the ink outline varied in thickness, the curves seemed to feel their way cautiously where they should have been bold ; in places the colour overran the line and everywhere in contrast to the opaque lithographic ink it was watery and transparent. It was no good.

Despondently Charles shut his drawing book and put his things together. Outside the Drawing School, steps led down to the Upper Quad past the doors of Brent's House—Frank's. Here he met Mercer.

" Hullo, been painting ? "

" Yes, if you can call it that."

" Let me see."

" No."

" Please."

" It's absolutely beastly. I hate it, I tell you. I'd have torn it up if I wasn't going to keep it as a humiliation to look at in case I ever begin to feel I know anything about art."

" You're always dissatisfied, Ryder. It's the mark of a true artist, I suppose."

" If I was an artist I shouldn't do things I'd be dissatisfied with. Here, look at it, if you must."

Mercer gazed at the open page. " What don't you like about it ? "

" The whole thing's nauseating."

" I suppose it *is* a bit ornate."

" There, my dear Mercer, with your usual unerring discernment you have hit upon the one quality that is at all tolerable."

" Oh, sorry. Anyway, I think the whole thing absolutely first-class."

" Do you, Mercer. I'm greatly encouraged."

" You know you're a frightfully difficult man. I don't know why I like you."

" I know why I like you. Because you are so extremely easy."

" Coming to the library ? "

" I suppose so."

When the library was open a prefect sat there entering in a ledger the books which boys took out. Charles as usual made his way to the case where the Art books were kept but before he had time to settle down, as he liked to do, he was accosted by Curtis-Dunne, the old new boy of last term in Brent's. " Don't you think it scandalous," he said, " that on one of the few days of the week when we have the chance to use the library, we should have to kick our heels waiting until some semi-literate prefect chooses to turn up and take us in ? I've taken the matter up with the good Frank."

" Oh, and what did he say to that ? "

" We're trying to work out a scheme by which

279

library privileges can be extended to those who seriously want them, people like you and me and I suppose the good Mercer."

" I forget for the moment what form you are in."

" Modern Upper. Please don't think from that that I am a scientist. It's simply that in the Navy we had to drop Classics. My interests are entirely literary and political. And of course hedonistic."

" Oh."

"Hedonistic above all. By the way, I've been looking through the political and economic section. It's very quaintly chosen, with glaring lacunae. I've just filled three pages in the Suggestions Book. I thought perhaps you'd care to append your signature."

" No thanks. It's not usual for people without library privileges to write in the Suggestions Book. Besides, I've no interest in economics."

" I've also written a suggestion about extending the library privileges. Frank needs something to work on, that he can put before the committee."

He brought the book to the Art bay ; Charles read " That since seniority is no indication of literary taste the system of library privileges be revised to provide facilities for those genuinely desirous of using them to advantage."

" Neatly put, I think," said Curtis-Dunne.

" You'll be thought frightfully above yourself, writing this."

" It is already generally recognized that I *am* above myself, but I want other signatures."

Charles hesitated. To gain time he said, " I say, what on earth have you got on your feet ? Aren't those house shoes ? "

Curtis-Dunne pointed a toe shod in shabby, soft black leather ; a laced shoe without a toe-cap, in surface like the cover of a well-worn Bible. " Ah, you have observed my labour-saving device. I wear them night and morning. They are a constant perplexity to those in authority. When questioned, as happened two or three times a week during my first term, I say they are a naval pattern which my father, on account of extreme poverty, has asked me to wear out. That embarrasses them. But I am sure you do not share these middle-class prejudices. Dear boy, your name, please, to this subversive manifesto."

Still Charles hesitated. The suggestion outraged Spierpoint taste in all particulars. Whatever intrigues, blandishments and self-advertisements were employed by the ambitious at Spierpoint were always elaborately disguised.

Self-effacement and depreciation were the rule. To put oneself explicitly forward for preferment was literally not done. Moreover, the lead came from a boy who was not only in another house and immeasurably Charles's inferior, but also a notorious eccentric. A term back Charles would have rejected the proposal with horror, but today and all this term he was aware of a new voice in his inner counsels, a detached, critical Hyde who intruded his presence more and more often on the conventional, intolerant, subhuman, wholly respectable Dr. Jekyll ; a voice, as it were, from a more civilized age, as from the chimney corner in mid-Victorian times there used to break sometimes the sardonic laughter of grandmama, relic of Regency, a clear, outrageous, entirely self-assured disturber among the high and muddled thoughts of her whiskered descendants.

" Frank's all for the suggestion, you know," said Curtis-Dunne. " He says the initiative must come from us. He can't go pushing reforms which he'll be told nobody really wants. He wants a concrete proposal to put before the library committee."

That silenced Jekyll. Charles signed.

" Now," said Curtis-Dunne, " there should be little difficulty with the lad Mercer. He said he'd sign if you would."

By lunch-time there were twenty-three signatories, including the prefect-in-charge.

" We have this day lit a candle," said Curtis-Dunne.

There was some comment around Charles in Hall about his conduct in the library.

" I know he's awful," said Charles, " but he happens to amuse me."

" They all think he's balmy in Brent's."

" Frank doesn't. And anyway I call that a recommendation. As a matter of fact, he's one of the most intelligent men I ever met. If he'd come at the proper time he'd probably be senior to all of us."

Support came unexpectedly from Wheatley. " I happen to know the Head took him in as a special favour to his father. He's Sir Samson Curtis-Dunne's son, the Member for this division. They've got a big place near Steyning. I wouldn't at all mind having a day's shooting there next Veniam day."

On Sunday afternoons, for two hours, the House Room was out of bounds to all except the Settle ; in their black coats and with straw hats under their arms the school scattered over the countryside in groups, pairs and occasional disconsolate single figures, for " walks ". All human habitations were barred ; the choice lay between the open down behind Spierpoint Ring

and the single country road to the isolated
Norman church of St. Botolph. Tamplin and
Charles usually walked together.

"How I hate Sunday afternoons," said
Charles.

"We might get some blackberries."

But at the door of the house they were
stopped by Mr. Graves.

"Hullo, you two," he said, "would you like
to make yourselves useful? My press has arrived. I thought you might help put it together." He led them into his room, where
half-opened crates filled most of the floor. "It
was all in one piece when I bought it. All I've
got to go on is this." He showed them a wood-
cut in an old book. "They didn't change much
from Caxton's day until the steam presses came
in. This one is about a hundred years old."

"Damned sweat," muttered Tamplin.

"And here, young Ryder, is the 'movable
type' you deplore so much."

"What sort of type is it, sir?"

"We'll have to find out. I bought the whole
thing in one lot from a village stationer."

They took out letters at random, set them,
and took an impression by pressing them, inked,
on a sheet of writing paper. Mr. Graves had
an album of typefaces.

"They all look the same to me," said Tamplin.

In spite of his prejudice, Charles was interested. "I've got it, I think, sir ; Baskerville."

"No. Look at the serifs. How about Caslon Old Style ? "

At last it was identified. Then Charles found a box full of ornamental initials, menu headings of decanters and dessert, foxes' heads and running hounds for sporting announcements, ecclesiastical devices and monograms, crowns, Odd Fellows' arms, the wood-cut of a prize bull, decorative bands, the splendid jumble of a century of English job-printing.

"I say, sir, what fun. You could do all sorts of things with these."

"We will, Charles."

Tamplin looked at the amateurs with disgust. "I say, sir, I've just remembered something I must do. Do you mind awfully if I don't stay ? "

"Run along, old Tamplin." When he had gone, Mr. Graves said, "I'm sorry Tamplin doesn't like me."

"Why can he not let things pass ? " thought Charles. "Why does he always have to comment on everything ? "

"You don't like me either, Charles. But you like the press."

" Yes," said Charles, " I like the press."

The type was tied up in little bags. They poured it out, each bagful into the tray provided for it in the worn oak tray.

" Now for the press. This looks like the base."

It took them two hours to rebuild. When at last it was assembled, it looked small, far too small for the number and size of the cases in which it had travelled. The main cast-iron supports terminated in brass Corinthian capitals and the summit was embellished with a brass urn bearing the engraved date 1824. The common labour, the problems and discoveries, of erection had drawn the two together ; now they surveyed its completion in common pride. Tamplin was forgotten.

" It's a lovely thing, sir. Could you print a book on it ? "

" It would take time. Thank you very much for your help. And now," Mr. Graves looked at his watch, " as, through some grave miscarriage of justice, you are not on the Settle, I expect you have no engagement for tea. See what you can find in the locker."

The mention of the Settle disturbed their intimacy. Mr. Graves repeated the mistake a few minutes later when they had boiled the kettle and were making toast on the gas-ring. " So at this moment Desmond O'Malley is sitting down to his first Settle tea. I hope he's enjoying it. I don't think somehow he is enjoying this term very much so far." Charles said nothing. " Do you know, he came to me two days ago and asked to resign from it ? He said that if I didn't let him he would do something that would make me degrade him. He's an odd boy, Desmond. It was an odd request."

" I don't suppose he'd want me to know about it."

" Of course he wouldn't. Do you know why I'm telling you ? Do you ? "

" No, sir."

" I think you could make all the difference to him, whether his life is tolerable or not. I gather all you little beasts in the Upper Dormitory have been giving him hell."

" If we have, it's because he asked for it."

" I dare say, but don't you think it rather sad that in life there are so many different things different people are asking for, and the only people who get what they ask for are the Desmond O'Malleys ? "

At that moment, beyond the box-room, the Settle tea had reached its second stage ; surfeited with crumpets, five or six each, they were starting on the éclairs and cream-slices. There was still a warm, soggy pile of crumpets left uneaten and according to custom O'Malley, as junior man, was deputed to hand them round the House Room.

Wheatley was supercilious. "What is that, O'Malley? Crumpets? How very kind of you, but I am afraid I never eat them. My digestion, you know."

Tamplin was comic. "My figure, you know," he said.

Jorkins was rude. "No, thanks. They look stale."

There was loud laughter among the third-year men and some of their more precocious juniors. In strict order of seniority, O'Malley travelled from boy to boy, rebuffed, crimson. All the Upper Dormitory refused. Only the fags watched, first in wonder that anyone should refuse crumpets on a cold afternoon, later with brightening expectancy as the full plate came nearer to them.

"I say, thanks awfully, O'Malley." They soon went at the under-school table and O'Malley returned to his chair before the empty grate, where he sat until chapel silently eating confectionery.

"You see," said Mr. Graves, "the beastlier

you are to O'Malley, the beastlier he'll become. People are like that."

4

Sunday, Sept. 28th. Choral. Two or three faints otherwise uneventful. Tried to do the initial and border for " The Bells of Heaven " but made a mess of it. Afterwards talked to Curtis-Dunne in the library. He intrigues me. With Frank's approval we are agitating for library privileges. I don't suppose anything will come of it except that everyone will say we are above ourselves. After luncheon Tamplin and I were going for a walk when Graves called us in and made us help put up his printing press. Tamplin escaped. Graves tried to get things out of me about ragging Dirty Desmond but without success. In the evening we had another rag. Tamplin, Wheatley, Jorkins and I hurried up to the dormitory as soon as the bell went and said our prayers before Dirty D. arrived. Then when he said," Say your dibs " we just sat on our beds. He looked frightfully bored and said " Must I repeat my instructions ? " As the other men were praying we said nothing. Then he said, " I give you one more chance to say your dibs. If you don't I'll report you."

We said nothing so off Dirty D. went in his dressing-gown to Anderson who was with the other house-captains at hot-air with Graves. Up came Anderson. "What's all this about your prayers?" "We've said them already." "Why?" "Because Tamplin got a late for taking too long so we thought we'd better start early." "I see. Well we'll talk about it tomorrow." So far nothing has been said. Everyone thinks we shall get beaten but I don't see how we can be. We are entirely in our rights. Geoghegan has just been round to all four of us to say we are to stay behind after First Evening so I suppose we are going to be beaten.

After First Evening, when the House Room was clear of all save the four and the bell for Hall had died away and ceased, Geoghegan, the head of the house, came in carrying two canes, accompanied by Anderson.

" I am going to beat you for disobeying an order from the head of your dormitory. Have you anything to say ? "

" Yes," said Wheatley. " We had already said our prayers."

" It is a matter of indifference to me how often you pray. You have spent most of the day on your knees in chapel, praying all the time, I hope. All I am concerned about is that you obey the orders of the head of the dormitory.

Anyone else anything to say ? Then get the room ready."

They pushed back the new men's table and laid a bench on its side across the front of the fireplace. The routine was familiar. They were beaten in the House Room twice a term, on the average.

" Who's senior ? You, I think, Wheatley."

Wheatley bent over the bench.

" Knees straight." Geoghegan took his hips and arranged him to his liking, slightly oblique to the line of advance. From the corner he had three steps to the point of delivery. He skipped forward, struck and slowly turned back to the corner. They were given three strokes each ; none of them moved. As they walked across the Hall, Charles felt the slight nausea turn to exhilaration.

" Was he tight ? "

" Yes, he was, rather. And damned accurate too."

After Hall, in the cloisters, O'Malley approached Charles.

" I say, Ryder, I'm frightfully sorry about tonight."

" Oh, push off."

" I had to do my duty, you know."

" Well, go and do it, but don't come and bother me."

"I'll do anything you like to make up. Anything outside the House, that is. I'll tell you what—I'll kick anyone else in another house, anyone you care to choose. Spratt, if you like."

"The best thing you can do is to kick yourself, Dirty Desmond, right round the cloisters."